"I want you to take your stuff out of here."

Slowly Duncan put away his pen. "What?"

"You heard me. We're done."

"What did I do?"

Mallory crossed the room until she was nearly nose-to-nose with him. "I did my part. I helped you, I let you into my house, I gave you my room when you asked me to. I even let you kiss me. And what did you do?"

"That's what I'd like to know." Duncan stood, eyes wide and innocent.

"Nothing you've told me since you got here has been the truth. You're completely made up. Every person you meet gets a different guy. You think I need a handyman? You play handyman. You think I need a boyfriend? You play that, too. What I want to know is, who is the real Duncan?"

"You want the real guy out the words. "Okay, how

He snaked around against him. Before breath, he crushed hers.

Dear Reader,

When I worked for law enforcement, I was always fascinated by the idea of a cop using someone's home as a surveillance post. In *Her Private Eye*, that fascination comes alive for Mallory and Duncan.

I'm particularly proud of this book, not only because it's my first Harlequin release, but because it's my master's thesis. Yes, you read that right! I'm grateful for the help of Lieutenant Patrick Picciarelli (NYPD Ret.), now president of Condor Investigations (who says stuff like this really happens); my dear D.M., Leslie Davis Guccione; Doctors Lee Tobin McClain, Mike Arnzen and Al Wendland; and Felicia Mason, Karolyn Duncan, Nalo Hopkinson, Catherine Mulvany, Jenny Andersen and the adjunct faculty and students of the M.A. in Writing Popular Fiction program at Seton Hill University.

I'd love to hear your thoughts on *Her Private Eye*. Drop me a line at P.O. Box 752, Redwood Estates, California, 95044, or visit me on the Web at www.shannonhollis.com.

Best,

Shannon Hollis

Her Private Eye
Shannon Hollis

For Karolyn —
This book wouldn't have
been what it is without
you.
Love,
Shannon

HARLEQUIN®

TORONTO • NEW YORK • LONDON
AMSTERDAM • PARIS • SYDNEY • HAMBURG
STOCKHOLM • ATHENS • TOKYO • MILAN • MADRID
PRAGUE • WARSAW • BUDAPEST • AUCKLAND

For Lori Senft, Cynthia Bates and Kathy Bates—
sisters in spirit as well as in law

ISBN 0-373-69131-9

HER PRIVATE EYE

Copyright © 2003 by Shelley Bates.

Visit us at www.eHarlequin.com

Printed in U.S.A.

1

"ELAINE, I'M NOT GOING to sleep with somebody just to make you and Mom happy." Mallory Baines cradled the phone between her shoulder and ear and selected a paintbrush. She dipped it in the can of paint and carefully applied Spanish Cream to the trim on the kitchen doorway. "Got that?"

"I never said you had to sleep with someone," her older sister protested. "Just go out on a date. Schedule a meeting. Something. I read an article in *Jane* about how to tell if someone has post-relationship depression, and you got a 'yes' on six of the twelve points. I'm looking out for you, here."

"Six out of twelve?" This was getting worse and worse. "I forbid you to analyze me with a list in *Jane*. Who is Jane, anyway?"

"Someone who gets more sex than you do, I'll bet."

"Ha-ha. I've been busy." Mallory inspected her free hand. Oops. She'd chipped another nail. "And breaking up with Jon was the best thing I ever did."

"It's been six months. For the last four you've been doing this 'I am woman, hear me drill' thing. You need to come out of that dump and behave like a civilized person."

"My house is not a dump," Mallory said, stung. "It's being renovated."

"With the three million from that stock, you could have a brand-new house in San Francisco and a ski chalet in Tahoe. But what do you do? You buy a Victorian nobody wants and spend twenty hours a day breaking your nails." Elaine paused ominously. "Fess up. You've got one of those leather tool belts, haven't you?"

Mallory decided to overlook that. "I don't want the kind of house everybody else has. I want to bring life back to this one. And do something completely on my own, for once." She dipped the brush again and smiled.

"I don't understand you. What do you call inventing that software and then putting your company on the New York Stock Exchange?"

"I did that with Jon. I think SpendSafe was the only reason we were together. Emotional independence is different, and you know it. And it doesn't include dates with whoever Mom's got up her sleeve for me this week."

"Have you told her about the guy across the street?"

Mallory rolled her eyes. "I don't tell Mom any more than she needs to know. She doesn't need to know about him."

"Single, responsible, home-owning... I've seen how he looks at you. And he helps you out, doesn't he?"

"Painting the dining room isn't a declaration of undying love."

"It is for some guys. And speaking of undying love, tell me what really happened between you and Jon—instead of the G-rated version."

Jon, the man who would not leave. Mallory owed her ex-fiancé no loyalty, but it was still hard to admit she could look so successful in public and be such a marshmallow inside. She'd spent too many years allowing people she loved to push her into molds that didn't fit her. Now she was a marshmallow in the process of renovating herself as well as this house.

"All right. I'll tell you. That last morning we had a meeting with the SEC, and we fought over whether the black Jimmy Choos went with my suit, or the navy Ferragamos. I could put up with him telling me which direction the plates were supposed to go in the dishwasher. I could even give in on black towels in the bathroom. But a woman's right to choose her shoes is sacred. I canceled the caterer that same morning."

"I always wondered what happened. It seemed so sudden."

"Now you know. Back to you."

"Okay, so maybe Mom and *Jane* together made me overreact. I have to admit, I do like your house. Or I will when it has floors. By the way, Mom told me over lunch that, in her opinion, you're substituting the house for the family you'll never have."

"Oh, please." Mallory almost leaned on the doorjamb, jerked upright and craned to look behind her. Not that another streak on her shorts would make much difference. "Know what she did last weekend?"

"I don't think I want to." Elaine paused, as if to brace herself. "What now?"

"She invited me over for dinner—and conveniently forgot to tell me she'd invited Jon."

"You may be over him, but I don't think she is. What did you do?"

"Walking out worked pretty well the last time, so I did it again. I think you're right. I think she's half in love with him herself. If I leave them alone often enough, maybe he'll propose."

Elaine laughed, but it ended in a sigh. "You're so brave. I could never have stood up to her like that."

"Yes, you could. If the two people who wanted to run your life the most ganged up on you over the artichoke hearts, you wouldn't just walk. You'd run."

"Come on, Mal. Mom just wants you to be secure and happy."

"I have all the security I'll ever need invested very nicely, thank you." The doorbell rang. "I've got to go. Someone's at the door."

"Call me later. I could use some pointers on how to just say no."

The bell rang again. She peered out of the beveled-glass window just as the guy on the porch raised his hand to the button again. "Can I help you?" she said through the glass.

"I'm looking for the person who owns this house," he told the door in a voice people usually reserved for the very old and deaf.

"Why?"

He reached into the left back pocket of his jeans as if

to retrieve some identification, frowned, then slapped a hand on the front pockets. He checked the right back pocket. Relief filled his face as he pulled out a slim black leather wallet.

She squinted to read it, gave up and flipped the dead bolt to open the door. "If you're trying to list it, it's not for sale."

He looked at her blankly, then glanced down as if to check that he had the right card behind the plastic cover. In doing so, he fumbled it and it fell facedown on the mat. He bent to retrieve it.

Oh, my.

Stop that, Baines, you shameless hussy.

"I'm not a Realtor." He straightened, dusted off the wallet and handed it to her. "I'm a private investigator. Duncan Moore." He smiled, a little-boy smile so appealing she caught herself smiling back. "And you are...?"

"Mallory Baines," she said absently as she read. The card confirmed what he'd said, so she memorized the phone number to check later, and returned it to him.

Then what he'd said actually registered. "Did I do something wrong?" She couldn't have. She hadn't been out of the house except to buy building supplies and food.

Her fingers tightened on the doorknob as icy apprehension splashed through her stomach. Jon. The fiancé scorned, the man who still couldn't accept that he'd lost control of his most valuable asset. Jon had sent this guy to tell her that she'd missed some microscopic detail during the initial public offering, that the

SEC was going to have her arrested and confiscate all the money. And then she'd be sorry for breaking their merger—er, engagement.

No, that couldn't be right. The IPO was finished. And anyway, they'd send the FBI for that, wouldn't they?

The detective was giving her the once-over, ending his perusal at the paint-speckled bandanna that held her uncontrollable hair off her face. "No, not at all. May I come in?"

"No, you may not." She closed the door slightly and wedged her body and one foot behind it. A guy with a cut that gave him a permanent case of bed head had no business staring at other people's hair. "What is this all about?"

He looked around as if there might be eavesdroppers hiding in the hydrangeas and then smiled at her again. It was hard not to remember he was a total stranger, that smile was so wickedly intimate. He had the kind of mouth good girls only dreamed about.

Stop that!

She had no business thinking about any kind of intimacy, much less looking at his mouth. Or his hands. Or his eyes. That kind of observation was what had drawn her into Jon's orbit two years ago, and look how *that* had turned out.

"I'm on the level," he said in a low voice. "Please?"

She dragged her attention back to the matter at hand. "Not until you tell me what you're here for. If it's got anything to do with my ex-fiancé, I'll ask you politely to leave."

"Don't know anything about him," he said. "I'm working a case and I need your help."

"My help?" She did a quick catalogue of her family and close friends. Nobody she knew had been doing anything scandalous lately. She stepped out onto the old-fashioned, wraparound porch and closed the door behind her.

He stepped back, almost to the stairs, and a board creaked under his foot. "Ma'am?"

When men start calling you ma'am, it's a sign you're turning into your mother. Although her mother wouldn't be caught dead in shorts and a camisole top. Well, Mallory worked hard. He was lucky she wasn't in bare feet and the T-shirt she slept in that said Save The Whales—They Make Me Look Thin.

"We can talk about it right here." She wasn't about to let a total stranger into the house, no matter how intriguing his eyes were. "If it's not Jon, what is it?"

He shoved both hands into his back pockets. His white cotton T-shirt pulled snugly across a broad chest. His arms and thighs were layered with muscle, and he had the kind of tan a man got by working outside.

"Unfortunately, I can't give you any of the details." He gave her an intense look from under long lashes.

Mallory's briskness evaporated as she sank slowly into that warm gaze. She'd never met anyone who gave his attention so fully to the person he was talking to. It made her skin prickle. She wondered what it would be like to make love with someone who was so totally aware of—

Mallory. Enough. He was a detective. It was his job to do things like that. He was probably looking for signs of drug use or confirming she wasn't wearing stolen jewelry.

Still she resisted the urge to check whether her buttons were done up. She could almost feel his concentration on her skin. This must be how Elaine felt all the time. She'd cornered the market on cheekbones and skinny blond looks, while Mallory got the genetic leftovers like Great-Grandma Baines's Edwardian bosom and Grandpa Morrison's freckles.

"May I call you Mallory?"

She hesitated. "All right."

"I need to enlist your help. Now this might seem a little unusual, but in reality it happens all the time." He gestured to the porch ceiling, and despite herself, Mallory looked up. "I'd like to ask if I could use one of the upstairs rooms."

She stared at him. This happened all the time? Did private detectives routinely move in with unsuspecting home owners all over America? "For what?"

His gaze caught hers and held it. "For surveillance. A stakeout. I'm working a fidelity case and the suspect has been seen in this neighborhood. I'd like to conceal myself so I don't spook the person. Your dormer windows are perfect for that."

"Those dormers are my personal space, Mr. Moore. I'm sorry, I'd love to help with truth and justice and all that, but not in my bedroom."

The moment the words left her mouth, she felt her indignation drain away and a flush creep up her cheeks. He broke eye contact, and she dragged a breath into lungs that suddenly felt constricted.

"Well then, would it be all right if I parked on the street in front of your house?"

His expression was warm and open, as if thoughts of her bedroom were furthest from his mind, but behind the warmth was something else. When working a roomful of potential investors, she had put on the same kind of smile and charm, and all the while she had been concentrating on extracting their cooperation and their money. This man certainly wanted her cooperation.

Mallory eyed him. He shifted from one foot to the other, and the board creaked again. She hoped it would hold. Among their other skills, private investigators were probably pretty good at lawsuits. He wore lace-up boots that looked as if they'd pounded their share of pavement. The hems of his stovepipe jeans were slightly frayed but clean.

A licensed investigator, huh? Anybody with a laser printer could produce cards and official-looking licenses in moments. There was a lot of discreet money in this neighborhood. He could be a scout for a burglary ring, scoping out all the houses from the safety of her curb.

Well, she'd hired and fired enough people in SpendSafe's brief but brilliant life to know if someone was conning her or not. He didn't seem underhanded, just determined. A nice woman would cooperate fully with the next thing to law enforcement. But until she was convinced his motives were what he said they

were, there was no law that said she had to give him
what he wanted, just because he asked.

"No," she said at last. "I don't want you in my
house. Or sitting in front of it." It felt odd delivering
that so bluntly, offering no reasons, making no ex-
cuses. It almost felt rude. Mallory returned to the door
and stood with one hand on the handle.

The determination faded from his eyes. The charm,
however, did not. He gave her a megawatt grin that
took her aback all over again. "I won't bother you.
You won't know I'm there. And I'm harmless." As if
to prove his point, he held both hands out, palms up.

"Not to whomever you're waiting for," she re-
torted.

Across the street, Blake Purdue came out of his
house, looked over at her and waved. When she
waved back, like a good neighbor would, he loped toward them. The detective had looked over his shoulder when he'd lost her attention, and now had gone
very still as he watched Blake come up the steps.

"Hey, Mallory." Blake sounded a little out of
breath, but his smile was wide and steady. "How's it
going? I heard Bank Lady last night on the way home
from work. It was pretty funny."

"Thanks. Has she made you change banks yet?"

"No." He looked a little embarrassed.

"That's okay. Luckily I didn't have to be a customer,
either, before I got the gig."

"Bank Lady?" The detective looked puzzled.

"She does radio commercials." Blake looked as

proud as if he were her agent. Mallory decided to step in.

"For Mid-City Bank. The work helps to keep groceries in the cupboards."

"Speaking of cupboards," Blake said, "do you want to set up a day to finish the painting?" Moments too late, he seemed to figure out what Duncan might be there for. "Oh. Sorry. Am I interrupting something?"

"That's okay. Mr. Moore was just leaving."

Mr. Moore didn't seem to be in any hurry. He stuck out his hand. "Duncan Moore. Nice to meet you."

"Blake Purdue." They shook hands. "You a friend of Mallory's?"

The detective grinned. "Not exactly. I was hoping to pick up some work around the place."

Mallory opened her mouth to correct him. His lashes flicked up and those green eyes flashed some kind of message at her. This man had chutzpah, along with the eyes and the mouth. First he wanted to move in. Now he was deliberately misleading her poor, unsuspecting neighbor.

And she was letting him.

Blake settled his weight on both feet. "I've been helping Mallory with the painting. The rest of the inside is pretty much finished up. You could try down at the union office."

The detective—if he was a detective—pulled one of his cards out of his wallet, its blank side toward Blake, and handed it to her. "If you change your mind, give me a call. Thanks for your time."

Automatically she pocketed it and watched as he

climbed into his car and drove away. She bet herself a dollar it didn't say *Duncan Moore, Private Detective*. It probably said *Painter*, or maybe *Professional Fibber*.

Misleading or not, at least he was interesting. Long-legged men with dazzling smiles didn't turn up on her doorstep every day of the week. Not that she cared, mind you. She was glad she'd stood up to him and ordered him off the property. A little practice at that was good for a woman.

So Elaine thought she was depressed and avoiding men, did she? Hardly. Why, the place was overrun with them. Contractors. Lost tourists. Blake. And now a private investigator. It wasn't as if Jon were her last hope. She could get involved with someone...*if* she wanted to. Her sex drive was temporarily in the shop, that was all.

Blake was still standing there, hope in his guileless blue eyes. She'd thought more than once that if you crossed the actor Greg Kinnear with a golden retriever, you'd get Blake Purdue. She smiled at him, and he smiled back, her knight in white picket fences. It wasn't his fault she didn't need a knight at the moment.

"I hope that guy wasn't giving you any trouble," he said. "I saw him through the window and it didn't seem like you wanted him around."

Now would be the time to share a little neighborhood gossip, invite him in for a cup of coffee and speculate about the fidelity case and who could be cheating on whom. But that would bring the conversation around to relationships, which was a little too close to sex, which was a topic she didn't want to get into with Blake Purdue under any circumstances.

She ran her thumb along the edge of the card in her pocket, and pulled it out.

Moore Investigations, it read. *Specializing in Lost People and Possessions.*

"No, he was just looking for work," she murmured.

And wondered what it was about Duncan Moore that would make a grown woman lie.

2

DUNCAN PARKED the car near the beach and slouched behind the wheel, frowning at the vast Pacific as the combers boomed in with the sound of distant thunder. The radio played a soft blues number, providing a melancholy background for his thoughts.

It was bad enough that he was facing several days of street surveillance—long, monotonous hours of sitting in the car, moving it once in a while just for entertainment.

But true to form, he'd managed to pick the one woman on the block who was best buds with his target. Good thing he hadn't told her the truth. He supposed he could have been more discreet, though, and not gaped at her as if he'd never seen creamy skin and world-class curves before. The thing to remember here was not the way her top had shown the world how God intended cleavage to look, but that he hadn't yet accomplished his goal. When he wrote up his report to his client, results would be the important thing, not his sexual responses to the neighbors.

His client, Barbara Mashita, the CEO of SiliconNext, had been crystal clear about the job. During their meeting on Monday, she'd told him, "Last week we lost sixty thousand dollars worth of memory modules.

Two weeks ago, it was seventy thousand. If we don't find out who's stealing them, we won't make our numbers this quarter. And if we don't make the numbers, the street hears about it, and the stock drops. I haven't worked eighteen-hour days for the past two years to let that happen." She had stopped pacing and dropped into her chair.

"So here I am. What am I looking for?"

A bag made of heavy pink plastic lay on her desk. She shook something out of it and handed it to him. "These."

He examined both sides of the little circuit board, no longer than the palm of his hand, and handed it back.

"Small, portable and high value. No wonder they're disappearing."

"Faster than the alimony I pay my ex. So here's what you're going to do." She pulled a sheaf of papers from a manila folder marked *Confidential*. "All I have is speculation and supposition, but you're going to make sense of it and get some answers." She shook her head, and her glossy black hair swung.

He and Barbara had been friends for years, and as she moved from company to company in Silicon Valley, picking up pay raises with every jump, she'd call him in when she needed help. When she went out on a limb with this start-up that employed mostly women and minorities and people looking to get off the welfare rolls, he'd watched with appreciation as SiliconNext took hold in the market and actually began to make waves in the computer industry. Successful clients meant checks that didn't bounce.

She handed him the paperwork. "That's a management matrix. Those are two anonymous e-mails, and this is a hallway conversation, written out as best the employee who heard it could remember. I need you to find out if the rumors are true, and get the parts back."

"Are you going to press charges?"

"I don't know yet. For the moment, let's concentrate on recovery before the financial impact is more than we can stand."

He got to his feet and held out a hand. "Will do."

She smiled, anxiety and relief in her eyes. "Thanks, Duncan. I know you'll give me your best. I'll have Melanie cut you an advance this afternoon."

She escorted him down the staircase to the modest lobby of SiliconNext's headquarters. The building was so new he could still smell the carpet. At the landing she paused. A huge fern extended its fronds over her head from a planter in the crook of the staircase, a dramatic touch that went a long way toward filling the space.

"So how are you these days?" she asked. "It's been weeks since we had lunch. Charmed any single female clients lately?"

He slid his hands into his pockets and looked up at the fern. "You offering?" She knew him too well to take him seriously, but she lightened up when he teased her.

"Get real. I'm married to this place. Anybody new in your life? You must meet lots of people on your cases."

"Yeah, cheating wives and gold-digging girlfriends who won't sign prenups. Just who I want to hit on."

"Stop evading. I've known you too long."

He shrugged. "Doesn't matter. I'm too busy anyway. Relationships take too much care and feeding. Besides, I've seen too many of 'em go bad. It skews your perception."

Behind the flippant questions, her dark eyes were concerned. He appreciated that. But he was too much in the habit of keeping the truth to himself.

"I'll call you as soon as I know anything. See you."

He loped down the rest of the stairs, aware she still stood above him. Empty space echoed all around them. As he pushed open the double glass doors, he ruthlessly squashed the flutter in his gut that threatened to become emotion. If a man kept his mind busy with theory and strategy, and planning the next step in an investigation, he wouldn't have room for the deadweight of regret that would only slow him down.

Gazing at the ocean now on this sunny June day, Duncan slouched deeper into the driver's seat of the silver coupe he'd chosen because it looked like half a dozen other kinds of cars. The giant waves rolled in with hypnotic regularity.

His first course of action had been to discreetly check out Barbara's operation, but he'd discovered there was no room for theft in the manufacturing process. Whoever was doing it was smart enough to find a loophole either before or after the parts went into production.

His second move was to spend a little time in the library of the *San Jose Mercury News* building, where he learned of two other computer companies that had had similar problems with theft. Unfortunately, they hadn't had enough evidence to prosecute. On the plus side, both companies contracted with Twenty-First Century Security, where his former partner was the Director of Operations.

If misery loved company, shared disgrace forged unbreakable friendships, which was why Geoff Rainer evidently felt no compunction about handing over his suspects' names. They hadn't panned out, but the names had produced the one thing no investigator could do without.

Phone records.

Duncan had given the names to the second thing no investigator could do without—his information broker. Brokers operated under the radar, in some cases illegally, but any P.I. worth his fee had access to one. Even with Geoff's help, there were too many avenues closed to the independent investigator otherwise.

Duncan's broker had come up with enough phone records to make even Duncan admit the guy was worth the outrageous amount of money he charged.

A suspicious number of those records had been calls made right here to Santa Rita, a town in a time warp. The only effect the eighties and nineties had had on its residents was that they noticed bell-bottoms were harder to get. They grew pot in the gardens of their mountain cabins and hung out at the local mushroom festival. Side-by-side with people who still wore black for Janis and Jimi and Jerry were the new breed of Internet geeks, renting cold spaces in gutted turn-of-the-century hotels, trying to make it big.

In such a polyglot of culture and technology, a smart crook would find it easy to blend in and disappear. No one would think twice about people coming and going from his house. In Santa Rita, it wasn't cool to ask.

Duncan flipped open his cell phone and speed-dialed Geoff's number. With this latest wrinkle, he could use another opinion.

"Twenty-first Century. Rainer speaking."

"Hey."

"Hey, yourself. Where are you?"

"Santa Rita. I think I found where those modules are going. My broker came up with some pretty interesting phone records from the names you gave me. A lot of them were to a number down here."

"I hate it when you get to use illegal sources and I don't. These people have a pretty shaky understanding of the term *profit sharing*, don't they? Do we know who the number belongs to?"

"I met the guy today." Duncan heard Geoff's feet slide off his desk and slam on the floor. His swivel chair squeaked so loudly Duncan heard that, too.

"What'd you do, take him down on the evidence of his phone records?"

"No. We don't make arrests anymore, remember?" The point was so sore with both of them that all they could do was joke about it. "I asked one of the neighbors if I could camp on the street for a while. Told her I was doing a fidelity case. If he's having the stuff delivered here by couriers from these companies, I'll know about it."

"That's risky, isn't it? Telling someone you're there?"

"Yeah, especially when the target came over to talk to her while I was standing there. He thinks I'm a contractor, drumming up business. He's probably got the hots for her and wanted to warn me off."

"Is she gorgeous, or what?"

"Yeah."

"Single?"

"No ring."

"Straight?"

"From the way he was looking at her, I'd say yeah."

"How come I never get these kinds of jobs?"

Duncan grinned. "Get back out on the street, and maybe you will."

"And then I wouldn't be around for you to call. Let me know if you need me."

Duncan flipped off the phone and dropped it back in his pocket. He wondered about Purdue, who might be using other companies' profits to pay his mortgage. He wondered about Mallory Baines, living alone in a neighborhood full of old, high-maintenance houses. Maybe she had inherited money, or maybe she was one of the few IPO rich left in Silicon Valley. Not that her bank account meant anything to him. Nor did the fact that those khaki shorts had shown him a pair of legs that would make a dead man sit up and take notice.

What was the matter with his mind? It kept returning to Mallory Baines instead of focusing on the target. She'd run him off. End of story. He didn't need to think about her. Didn't need to let the camera eye of memory ramble lazily over the shadowy curves of the most spectacular cleavage he'd seen in months. Years. Cleavage he could bury his imagination in and die a happy man.

Duncan straightened in the driver's seat and commanded his body to stop what it was doing and settle down. Through the open window, the breeze off the ocean was soft but steady, with a coolness that told him the marine layer hiding off the coast was going to steal in within the next hour to make visibility difficult and warmth impossible. He should have brought a jacket. He should have asked her if he could use her bathroom before she ran him off.

On the radio, the deejay ended his set and cut to the commercial. A woman with an uptight persona, precise diction, and an air of exasperation spoke out of the dash speakers. With a little shock of recognition, he realized he'd just heard that honey-on-toast voice within the past hour.

"Last week I was in the bank and let me tell you, it was no picnic. After thirty minutes of standing in the teller line, I was so well acquainted with the man behind me that we started having an affair. That's when I decided to move my accounts to Mid-City Bank." The commercial segued to a list of rates and terms, and Duncan turned it off.

So Mallory was the Bank Lady. If the radio gig kept food in the cupboards, how did she pay the rest of her bills? He'd give a lot to know how close Mallory Baines was to Purdue. He'd bet the guy had a network of accomplices, draining the profits out of other companies as well as SiliconNext. Maybe Mallory Baines wasn't IPO rich at all. It wouldn't be the first time in his experience that a pretty woman saw the profit margins in a life of crime. Maybe at this moment they were having a drink and talking over their little scam. Maybe she'd blown his little bit of deception by showing Purdue his business card.

Well, let her. He was on a fidelity case, wasn't he? His real purpose was safe.

The temperature began to drop as the sun went down and the fog moved toward shore. A lucky break. He rolled up the window to conserve the warmth inside the car, and by the time he'd driven quietly to a stop behind a screen of bushes in front of Mallory Baines's neighbor's house, visibility had dropped to ten feet. He could no longer see Purdue's place. The guy could be building his own computers and shipping them from his garage, for all Duncan could tell in the gloom.

He waited an hour, then two, but no cars passed him on the quiet street. When a glance at the illuminated dial of his watch told him it was after nine, Duncan contemplated sneaking over and having a look in the windows. Two men could pass in Purdue's yard and never know it.

For a moment, the mist shifted and he saw movement to his left, in the trees. The adrenaline leaped in his veins. He was the watcher here—he couldn't allow someone to sneak up on him. He opened the door and slipped out. No overhead lights came on to give him away; he'd disabled the switch the day he'd bought the car. Crouching low, he crept between the bushes, moving from tree to tree, listening after each cautious step to make up for his compromised sight.

A stick snapped. He turned and grabbed, and his prey squealed and kicked him on the shin.

"Let go of me!" He recognized that voice an instant after he realized the thrashing shape in his arms was nowhere near the size of Blake Purdue.

"Ms. Baines. Mallory. It's me, Duncan Moore." He let her go and she leaped back, her face a pale oval in the dark.

"What are you doing? I told you not to stay here!"

"I have a job to do, ma'am. I'm legally parked on municipal property. I saw something move in your yard and I got out to investigate. Sorry I grabbed you. I thought it might be an intruder."

"You're the intruder." She pushed her hair back with one hand and pressed the other to her ribs. "I'm half tempted to call the cops. You scared me to death."

"Most women would have called them from inside the house. If it hadn't been me you might have been in real trouble."

She made a derogatory noise and dismissed that. "I was looking for my cat. She's usually on the back porch, but this time she wasn't, so she's probably in Blake's yard ag—" She cut herself off and breathed in through her nose, then out.

Puffs of fog swirled around them, leaving cool trails

on his bare arms, and deadening sound. It created the illusion that they were in a small, dark closet, where the things they said would stay secret.

"You must be pretty good friends if you're sharing custody." Friendly enough to feed the cat, he wondered, or friendly enough to sleep over, and maybe sell a few memory modules on the side?

"Don't talk to me about custody. Kiko isn't even mine. She belongs to my former fiancé. I can't help it that she's got a thing for men."

"Nothing wrong with that."

"There is if you live with me."

Uh-oh. Maybe he'd been wrong in his conversation with Geoff. "Why?"

"Around here, men are good for one thing, and one thing only."

His grin broke free, and he couldn't keep it out of his voice. "Is that an offer?"

It was too dark to see her face, but her glare was evident in the grittiness of her tone. "Trust a man to think of that first. I meant construction."

"Can't help you there. But I can provide some security if you let me hang around."

"I already told you no. I don't need security. What I need is a little peace and quiet, without guys around expecting things they don't deserve."

He'd been up-front about what he wanted, Duncan thought, as he watched her stalk away into the mist. Moments later he heard her climb the stairs to the house. He'd give a helluva lot to know what Purdue expected from his pretty neighbor.

3

SOMETHING'S WRONG.

Mallory started awake from a dream about leafy bushes and naked skin and lay still, her heart jumping.

Ever since she'd moved in, the house had made odd noises. A shudder at midnight. A scrape at three in the morning. She'd given up going down with a flashlight and a two-by-four to investigate because she'd never found anything to account for the sounds. She'd even had all the pipes replaced, in case the ancient plumbing was at fault, and eventually chalked it up to living in the earthquake zone.

Somewhere deep in the house, something shivered. An icy sound, like glass breaking.

Fear jabbed her stomach. If only she had a two-by-four. Or a burly roommate. Or an upstairs phone extension.

Get out of the house.

No way was she going down there. She wasn't that stupid. She flung off the covers and pulled on a pair of sweatpants under her T-shirt. The window creaked as she swung it open, and she winced. If she could just get over to Blake's, she could call the cops from there.

The roof shakes were rough and cold under her

bare feet, curling up at the edges and ready to trip her. Crablike, she moved along the roof to where it broke for the front porch, and thanked heaven for the architect who had designed the latticework to double as a fire escape. She dropped to the porch as silently as she could and raced down the steps.

"Oof!"

She ran smack into a big, dark, scary body. An accomplice. Out to kill. She dragged in a breath to scream.

"Mallory, what's going on? Are you okay?" A pair of strong, warm arms wrapped around her and she sagged against him, her knees suddenly turning to rubber.

"Blake, thank God. You've got to—"

"Not Blake. It's me. Duncan."

She suddenly realized her arms were wrapped around the man's waist in a death grip, and her cheek was pressed to his shirt. Heat came off him like a force field, and she flushed from the crown of her head to her toes. The flush receded, and left her cold and shaky. She tried to push away, but he wouldn't let her.

"Tell me what's wrong."

"Are you still here? Let me go. I've got to get away."

"From what? I saw you come out on the roof. You crazy woman, you could have been killed. Is the house on fire?"

"We could both be killed while you stand here talking!" She struggled, but somehow the danger didn't seem so imminent when she felt so warm.

There was a burglar in the house. She needed to get to Blake's and call the cops.

Didn't she?

She sagged against him, shivering and gasping for breath. His hand came up and he stroked her back, long strokes, from shoulder blade to waist. Calming her. She began to relax.

"Tell me what happened. Please." His voice was getting ragged.

"A noise woke me up. Like glass breaking. I think someone's inside."

His palm on her spine lost its comforting gentleness and went rigid. "I want you to go to my car and lock yourself inside it. Okay? It's parked right there, on the street."

"I need to go to Blake's and phone the police."

"Mallory, I am the police." He paused. "Or the next best thing. I'm going to search your house. Hear me?"

"You can't get in. It's locked."

"Where's the spare key?"

"There isn't one."

"Okay. If you can get down, I can get up. Now, go." He gave her a little shove, and she took a couple of running steps.

"Now who's crazy?"

But he didn't answer. He tested the lattice with a firm grip, then started to climb. In seconds he was up on the porch roof, then through her bedroom window. She turned and stumbled through the yard to where the car was parked behind her plumbago bushes, and climbed inside. She made sure every door was locked, and huddled there, arms wrapped tight around her body.

Long minutes passed. She couldn't see anything but her bedroom dormers above the trees, and they remained dark, revealing nothing. She glanced around the interior of the car. A notebook lay on the center console, its pages open to what looked like a list of numbers and letters.

She squinted. They were license plate numbers.

She imagined him sitting out here watching for his cheating husband or wife or whomever, writing down the plate numbers of every car that drove by. He must be what he said he was. Nobody would do such a thing for fun.

Something tapped on the window, and she jumped about a foot.

Duncan leaned down. "It's just me. Unlock the door."

She flipped the lock and he slid behind the wheel. He looked over at her and she cringed. She must look like the Wild Woman of Borneo, hair sticking out every which way, in a wrinkled T-shirt that made it obvious she wore nothing underneath. Thank goodness it was dark. She crossed her arms over her obnoxious chest and made herself as small as possible. "Well?"

"There's nothing. I checked every window and there's no sign of broken glass anywhere. I went through all the rooms, looked under all the furniture."

"Closets?"

"Those, too. Nice job you're doing on the house, by the way."

"Thanks. I'm sure it sounded like glass. And that was after the noise that woke me up."

"I'll check the basement if you tell me where the door is."

She shook her head. "This is the San Andreas Fault zone, remember? We don't do basements."

"Right. I keep forgetting I'm not in Colorado anymore." He reached over and took her hand. For a moment she was too surprised to pull away. The warmth of his hand surrounded her chilled fingers, and made the rest of her body seem even colder by contrast. The dregs of the adrenaline finished their work until she could no longer control her shivering.

"You're in shock. Come on. I'm going to take you into the house."

"I don't want to go in there."

"I checked it out completely. It was probably just a little tremor that rattled your windows. But to make you feel better, I'll stay with you for a bit."

A sensible, modern woman who put companies on the stock exchange would have refused his help and gone to a motel for the night. But that woman hadn't felt the warmth of Duncan Moore's hand or heard the gentle concern in his voice. His top priority, for the time being, was no longer the license plates or somebody's runaway spouse or what he was being paid to do.

She was his priority. She, Mallory Baines. It was impossible to resist.

"Come on."

He held her hand and led her in through the now open back door. While she took a hot shower to warm up, he waited out in the hallway to scare off any burglars that might still be in residence. And when she'd climbed into her thickest, warmest, ugliest sweats and come to the bedroom door to thank him, he put both hands on her shoulders and looked into her face.

"You'll be okay to sleep?"

"I think so. You didn't have to do this, you know."

He was silent for a moment, his hands flexing gently on her upper arms, as if making sure she was really there. "I was in the neighborhood anyway."

The buttery light from her bedside lamp created a shadow down his side through the partially open door, but didn't illuminate his face. He began to move away. She covered one of his hands with her own and he stilled, as if the touch had surprised him.

"Where are you going?" Her voice was a little too high, a little too fast.

"I'm going to camp on your couch downstairs. If these noises reoccur, I want to be a little closer than out on the street, on the far side of the enchanted forest."

Somehow his fingers tangled with hers, and he tugged her a little closer. Or maybe her feet moved that tiny step by themselves, so she stood between his boots.

He smelled so good, like clean, warm cotton and sweat and pine needles. She only meant to give him a hug, to say thank-you, just between friends. But his arms went around her before she could take another breath, and his mouth found hers.

His lips were hot, his mouth silky and unyielding all at once. She opened her mouth to him, and he took the invitation, hard and fast. Sparks shot along her veins to pool in a molten ball low in her belly.

Somebody made a throaty sound, and he jumped as if there were a growling animal behind him. She felt the tension in his hands as he set her away from him, a tension at odds with the way her body had melted under them.

"Sorry," he said roughly. "That was way out of line."

And he left her there, desire zinging helplessly in her bloodstream, while her skin cooled with the finality of rejection.

She heard his boots on the stairs, and listened for the closing door that would tell her he'd decided to cut and run from the Wild Woman of Borneo. But instead, she heard him go into the great room. The couch sighed as he sat heavily on its overstuffed cushions.

She went into her room, closed the door and locked it. Then she crawled under the covers, pulled them over her head, and wished that the San Andreas would live up to its reputation and suck her down into a crevasse before she had to face Duncan Moore, finder of lost libidos, in the morning.

STUPID, STUPID, STUPID! What the hell had he been thinking, taking advantage of a woman in shock?

Duncan attempted to clean up with a washcloth and a sinkful of hot water, since he wasn't sure how well a strange man in her shower would go over with his hostess this morning.

He'd lain awake on the couch most of the night, wishing he could turn back time and undo those few dizzy seconds when he'd finally discovered that her lips were as soft and inviting as they looked. There was something about this woman that made him want to reach out and touch something. Hair. Clothes. Skin. Mouth.

Well, he'd messed up royally now. If anything would send her running to Purdue as she had wanted to last night, it would be this. Duncan had only been able to stop her because she'd been too scared to think straight. Cover story or no, he might as well go back to Barbara Mashita and admit defeat.

He scrubbed himself mercilessly, trying to keep most of the water in the sink and not on the floor. He had no business thinking about how soft and warm she was in his arms. The last time he'd thought about that was the time he'd learned the definition of betrayal—the hard way.

He wiped water out of his eyes with the heel of one hand. He could not let himself be distracted by a woman involved in a case. Six years ago he'd thought it was possible to keep the personal and the professional sides of his life separate.

What a fool he'd been. Trusting Amy Friedman had done nothing but lead to betrayal.

Duncan folded the washcloth. His screwup had cost

Geoff and him their jobs. After their lieutenant had collected their shields and weapons, it was permanent vacation time. They had headed west and Duncan, at least, had tried not to let the anger destroy him. Geoff hadn't been quite so successful, but A.A. seemed to be helping.

Duncan could look at Mallory Baines's curves and skin. No problem. But he couldn't touch. Not even by accident. He was not going to jeopardize another case, especially when he knew so little about her.

He mopped up the sink, hung his towel over the shower rail and dressed swiftly. In the middle of a quick trim of his nails, he nearly dropped his Swiss Army knife when he heard domestic sounds from the direction of the kitchen. The rush of water, the clink of glass. The smell of freshly ground coffee filled the house.

So much for trying to be quiet and considerate. Just his luck, she was an early riser. There was no putting it off now.

He should leave. But Barbara wasn't paying him for that. And he wasn't a quitter, even when a smart guy would cut his losses and go. He had to save the situation.

Groveling sometimes worked. He could do that.

He entered the kitchen quietly. Her back was to him as she stood at the counter, watching coffee drip into the pot. Her denim skirt stopped four inches above her knees, revealing those legs. That was bad. The hem of her T-shirt rode low on her hips, and covered everything else. That was good. She'd pulled her hair up into a twist, and held it with one of those hinged clips with all the teeth in them that were popular with women these days. A mug with the Tasmanian devil creating a tornado on one side, sat by the coffeemaker.

Uh-oh. One mug. It was a safe bet it wasn't for him.

Groveling time. "Mallory."

She looked up and color washed her cheeks in waves. She turned hastily away. "Good morning." Her voice was muffled, her head bent.

"I want to apologize for last night."

She hunched her shoulders a little more. "How many movies have I watched where the guy wakes up in the morning and says that? Is that something men learn in school?"

"I don't know about other guys. I meant it. I took advantage of you. If you want me to go, I will."

"How was searching my house and then staying to make sure I was okay taking advantage?" She picked up the mug, filled it, and hid the lower half of her face behind it as she sipped.

He dared to feel a little optimistic. "You know what I mean. After that."

"The part where I threw myself into your arms?" Her cheeks were flushed, but she forged on anyway. "I'm the one who should apologize to you."

Here was a twist he hadn't expected. "You were scared and in shock. But that doesn't excuse my kissing you. It won't happen again." He'd make damn sure of that.

Her shoulders sagged a little. He was used to reading people, watching for the involuntary movements that told him more than they said. In this case, he couldn't tell whether it meant disappointment or relief.

"I hope these noises don't happen again." Time to change the subject before she overheated from blushing. "I'd really like to stay on, though. In case they do."

The color faded from her face. "You just don't give up, do you? I'm surrounded by men who will not leave."

To his relief and surprise, she reached into the cupboard and pulled out a black mug with a gold SpendSafe logo.

"I wouldn't get far in this business if I did give up. But I'll leave if you want me to." Then come up with another plan. He wasn't sure what, though.

"I hope he's worth it," she said.

A mouthful of coffee went down the wrong way, and he coughed. When his throat cleared, he looked up. "Who?" She couldn't be on to him. Impossible. He'd given nothing away. Or had he?

"Your cheating husband. Or wife, or whatever."

Jeez, Moore, don't be so jumpy. "Wife. Yeah, it's worth it. But I'll do double duty in return. Free security services, bodyguard duty, whatever you need."

Inexplicably she blushed again. "All right, all right. You can stay. But I'm under construction in here. Don't get in the way."

"I won't. Now, about your dormer windows."

"I have lots of windows. Do you have to have those?"

"They're the best for my purposes."

"Great." She muttered something about men and bedrooms, but since she'd turned and spoken to the coffeepot, he didn't catch most of it.

"I won't disturb anything. All I need is the window."

"All right. But if I start feeling weird about it, out you go."

"Deal. As I said before, you won't even know I'm here."

"I doubt that."

He gave a sigh of relief. How many cases gave him an observation post made-to-order? Or one that enabled him to watch not only his suspect but a possible connection to him?

Or was it more than that? Did this lightness in his chest have more to do with being back on an even keel with this woman he'd met only yesterday than it did about achieving his goal?

That was a bad sign. *Focus,* he told himself sternly.

He followed her up the staircase to check out the room in daylight, but before he'd climbed two steps he realized just how difficult this job was going to be. Her long, smooth legs were at eye level. The temptation to reach out and touch one of her ankles with one hand, just to see if her skin was as soft as it looked, was almost overwhelming.

But he resisted it. Not only would she run screaming to the cops, or worse, Blake Purdue, she'd probably kick him. With the height and pitch of these stairs, the landing could be fatal.

He followed her into the bedroom, and no matter how he tried to focus, all thoughts of his case sizzled into oblivion like water on a griddle.

The sun coming through the glass backlit the wild ripples of her hair and turned her well-worn T-shirt transparent. He could distinctly see the dusky circles of her nipples as the weight of her breasts pressed them into it. How thin could a bra get and still do its job? he wondered, dazed. For several seconds of unexpected pleasure, his gaze traced the profile of her lush curves to the tips of her nipples, down the full lower curve and back to her rib cage.

She turned to face him, stepping into the shadow, and he swallowed. This was worse than last night. First touching, now looking. How much could one man be expected to resist for the sake of justice?

He walked to the window and looked out, fighting down his rioting impulses. He tried to concentrate instead on the view of Blake Purdue's garage and back door. This window was perfect. Every time Purdue stuck his nose out of his house for any reason, Duncan would be there to watch it. Every time someone came to visit, he'd be at the window with his camera and its 400mm zoom lens. Every time Mallory Baines talked to or about Purdue, Duncan would be there to overhear.

He had to resist, and not for the sake of justice. For his own self-respect.

"This is great." His responses once more under control, he turned back to Mallory. "If it's okay, I'll go get a few personal things, and be back later."

"Fine. I hope the couch was comfortable. That's where you'll be sleeping."

He couldn't stop a glance at the bed against the far wall. It was a haven of femininity, with tall posts and draperies of gauzy fabric forming a canopy over a duvet in jewel colors. It was something straight out of *A Thousand and One Nights*.

Don't think about the nights.

"Sounds good." He swallowed again. "My hours can be strange."

She shook her head. "I'll do things the way I always do them. If we run into problems we'll work them out."

"Just think of me as furniture." And he wouldn't think of her as anything but a suspect.

Deliberately he turned his back on the bed and followed her out of the room. He had just enough time to race home, throw a few things into a bag, and be back to greet anyone leaving the early shift and driving to Blake's.

Duncan had to remember his primary objective was to watch Blake Purdue, not the lovely Mallory Baines. If he had the sense God gave an oyster, he'd ignore her as much as possible and just figure out the drop schedule and who the major players were. He'd fill his mind with the case until there was no room left for women with peachy skin and luscious lower lips made for kissing.

There was no room in this case for emotional involvement. None at all.

4

SOME DAYS all you could do was pick up the phone and call your best friend.

Carly Aragon answered her cell phone on the second ring. "Hey, *mija*. I was just going to call you. What's up?"

Mallory smiled at the endearment. When Carly had been her executive administrator at SpendSafe, she'd been a friend from the very first day. Mallory was glad the friendship had outlasted the job.

"If I told you, you wouldn't believe me. When are we getting together?"

"Given the exciting choices of finishing an Economics assignment or going grocery shopping, I hope it's soon. Tell you what—we should go to that new casino up in the Valley. I hear they book really great music in there. We could dance. Drink. Scout for men."

Mallory laughed. "Dancing and drinks are great. Men are the last thing I need."

"*Cara*, you just keep telling yourself that. All the more for me."

"I'm serious. Besides the Man Who Will Not Leave, I've got contractors, I've got Blake, and now I've got a private detective."

"No way."

"He's sleeping on my couch."

"Mallory Baines. Do you know where liars go?"

"I swear. He says he's watching for a cheating wife or husband or something, and he's using my bedroom window."

"But he sleeps on the couch. Is there something you're not telling me? Like you signed up with the Sisters of Perpetual Virginity when I wasn't looking?"

"Very funny. You know what my priorities are right now. But I've got to admit, he brought all his pheromones in with him and, boy, are they flying around in the air."

"This sounds promising. Don't waste a perfectly good man. Use those pheromones, *chica*."

"For all I know, he could be married with kids." This had not occurred to her before, but it could be one explanation for the abrupt way he'd disappeared into the night. She felt more of a fool than ever. "Never mind. You and I are going out on the town. Friday. I'll pick you up."

"Right. And I'll wear my red leather bustier. It's got a money-back guarantee."

"For what? Not to let you down in moments of stress?"

"No, silly. To keep the male attention right where it belongs. Pheromones have nothing on this thing. If it works, I'll let you borrow it."

Mallory rolled her eyes as she hung up the phone. Carly never believed her when she said she was too focused on her home to deal with a relationship right now.

But when she remembered how Duncan's arms had felt around her, she could almost reconsider.

Almost.

She tidied up the bedroom and hustled all personal objects, such as her teal-green lace bra and a bunch of photographs of Elaine and Matt's last trip to Florida, out of sight. Then she moved an armchair from the hall to the window. She sat in it to test the view. He'd said he was here to look for a car, but it seemed odd for anyone to sit in one place at the end of a dead-end street waiting for it. If she were in that silver two-door, she'd have been cruising alleys and drifting up and down all the roads in the area.

A small black pickup truck rolled into view and parked in front of the empty rental on the corner. A young man got out of it and walked toward Blake's house. She watched, idly. This must be a friend of Blake's. He had lots of them, dropping in at all hours. It certainly wasn't the cheating spouse. The kid couldn't be more than twenty. He crossed the lawn to Blake's back door, and before he could even raise a hand to knock, the door opened and he slipped inside. A moment later the door opened again and the man came out, jogged to his truck and drove away. Then Blake opened his garage door and drove off to work.

Men sure weren't much for sitting down with a cup of coffee and catching up on the latest gossip, were they?

She went downstairs to the great room, and popped the lid off the can of Spanish Cream. She was just getting ready to start when the doorbell rang.

"Mal, I have to talk to you," her sister greeted her when she opened the door. "It's an emergency."

Mallory's heart started to gallop, and she pressed a hand to her chest. "What is it? Did something happen to Kevin or Holly?" She looked out at the minivan parked at the curb, but there was no blood or broken glass. There were no kids, either.

"Of course not. They're at swim camp. I mean a personal emergency. A life decision."

Mallory led Elaine into the great room, put the lid back on the paint and sank into the easy chair. "What kind of life decision? Does Matt want another baby or something?"

"Good Lord, no." Elaine pushed at the air with both hands, as if to make the idea go away, then rubbed the frown lines between her eyes. "I had my tubes tied after Kev, remember? No, I've been thinking of expanding my horizons. Revitalizing my creativity. Do you have any more commercials coming?"

Mallory struggled to follow the grasshopper jumps of her sister's conversation. "We taped one last week that should start airing in July. I've got a corporate video lined up, but I'm not scheduled to do anything for the bank until next month. Their writer went to Pixar and they're having trouble finding someone."

"Really?" Elaine paused, then took a breath. "I've been thinking of getting back into journalism now that the kids are in school."

"Oh, that kind of life decision. You had me worried there for a second. Are you going to freelance?"

"I don't know yet. I thought I'd send some clips

around, but...since this writer has quit and all, do you think they'd look at something of mine?''

Mallory tried to keep her face still so her sister wouldn't mistake astonishment for insult. Elaine? Write for radio?

''Mal?''

She changed position in the chair to give herself a second to think. ''I'm just surprised. It—it's not like the articles you were doing, is it?''

''Maybe I want to do something different. I was pretty good. Do you think I have a chance?''

''Have you ever written a commercial script?''

''Of course not. But how hard can it be? The spots are thirty seconds long.''

Mallory thought of the writer's moans of despair, and how the lines sometimes got rewritten and shoved into the recording booth practically as she was reading them.

''Tell you what. I have a couple of old ones here. You can get the format from them, write one up and I'll read it. If it's—'' she almost said good, then changed her mind ''—something they can use, I'll take it in for Rich to look at. All right?''

''That'd be great. You're such a darling.''

''Here, let me hunt around for them.'' She picked up a pile of books, then riffled through a stack of mail-order magazines and bids for the kitchen. ''I know they're here somewhere.''

''Ready for lunch?'' Elaine picked up the catalogues. ''It's probably hunger that's giving me this headache. I've been down at the mall all day, hitting up the summer sales. Not all of us can afford to pay full price for things."

"Oh, right, like I ever do." Mallory sorted through the stack of paper that sat on the floor next to the computer. "There are some behaviors you just can't change."

"If I had your bucks, I'd change a few," Elaine said.

"Here they are." Mallory pulled the scripts out of the pile, the pink paper signifying the final version. Or as final as versions got before she actually went into the booth. "I meant to file these, but since things started rolling with the house, everything else in my life has gone on hold."

Elaine tucked them into her backpack-shaped purse with the catalogues and wandered in the direction of the kitchen. "What have you got in here?"

Her mind went blank with panic. Were there two mugs sitting on the counter, or not? No one was supposed to know Duncan was here. His case might depend on it.

"Hey, Elaine, why don't you get comfy and I'll make lunch?" She stepped in front of her and gestured toward the couch. "You can start reading those over, get a feel for what Richard's looking for."

Elaine smiled fondly and stepped to one side. "With the kids gone, I've got all kinds of time to read them over at home, make notes, that kind of stuff. I only get one chance at this. I want to make sure I give them the best I have."

"So you can't start soon enough. Sit down and relax. I'll call you when I've got lunch rustled together."

Elaine shrugged. "All right, all right. You're the expert. Let me know if I can help."

With a sigh of relief, Mallory hustled into the kitchen and glanced around for incriminating evidence. No second mug. Disaster averted.

Still, he could come back at any second. Listening for the sound of his car engine took away her appetite. While Elaine washed her hands after eating, Mallory piled the dishes in the sink and ran water into it.

"Hey, Mal," her sister called from the bathroom.

"Yes?"

"Did you have company last night?"

"What?" Mallory froze, the dishcloth taut between her hands.

"This towel over the shower rail is damp."

The bathroom! Duncan had used the bathroom this morning. The blood drained out of her face. "I—oh, that was me."

Elaine stuck her head out of the doorway. "You have a bathroom upstairs."

"It—the one up there doesn't have a tub. You know, sometimes you just feel like having a bath."

"I wish I had that luxury. But with two kids it's hard enough getting two minutes to put my makeup on. D'you have any aspirin?"

"Should be some in the cabinet." Mallory relaxed her grip on the cloth and stuffed it down the throat of a glass.

"Mallory?" Elaine called a moment later.

"Yes?"

"Why is there a Swiss Army knife in here? And such a big one, too."

"A what?" Mallory's lungs stopped functioning. "What did you say?"

Elaine walked out with a swing in her hips, pulling out implements one by one, as if she were playing "he loves me, he loves me not."

"Two knives, a nail clipper, tweezers, a corkscrew, ooh, even a little pair of pliers. And look at this engraving. D.R.M. Now, who could that be? Looks like little sister is hiding a bi-i-i-g secret."

Mallory gaped at the knife, Elaine's shame-on-you grin and the bathroom door. "Where did that come from?"

"That's what I'd like to know. You bad girl. Just who is D.R.M.? Does Jon know? More important, does Mother?"

"I swear, Elaine, I didn't know that was there. Maybe the previous owners left it."

"Right. Come on, you can tell me. It's the guy across the street, isn't it? What's his name? Don? Dave? Are you two a hotter item than I thought?"

"Of course not." She wished her lungs and her brain would start working normally. "His name's Blake. Stop pushing me at him. You're as bad as Mom."

"I am nothing like our mother," Elaine said. "But you know how sensitive she is about you being single."

Sensitive? Their mother was phobic about it. To her, being single was the worst plague a woman could bear. If you were a single woman without children, you might as well be dead, and Dorothy wasn't about to let that be Mallory's fate, no matter what Mallory had to say about it. Her chest seized up at the thought of what her mother would say if she got the tiniest hint she was harboring a man as unsuitable as Duncan Moore in her bedroom...not to mention spying on other people's errant spouses.

Elaine gave her a measured look, the same look she'd given Mallory over the headless Princess Leia action figure when they were kids. Mallory hadn't been able to come up with a believable story then, either. But before she could do more than take a breath, a voice called from the front door.

"Hey, I'm back."

She closed her eyes briefly and ordered herself to stay calm. If Duncan Moore wanted to remain incognito, he should know better than to show up when there was a soccer-mom van parked out front.

He strolled into the kitchen as if he'd not only been there before, but he'd helped build it, too. He stuck out a hand.

"Hi, I'm Duncan."

Elaine actually batted her eyes at him. "I'm Mallory's sister, Elaine."

"Nice to meet you."

Mallory saw his gaze catch on the Swiss Army knife lying on the counter.

"Ms. Baines, I'll need you to call the lumberyard. They had a problem with me using your account this morning, so the order's on hold until they hear from you."

"Oh. Sure. No problem."

"Are you working for Mallory?" Elaine asked. "What do you do?"

"A little of everything," Duncan said with a smile. "Painting, finish work, you name it."

"Your initials wouldn't be D.R.M., would they?" Elaine smiled back. Then she shot Mallory an "I've got you now" look.

Mallory felt like sliding to the floor and then banging her head on the cupboard door. As their grandmother would say, Elaine had more guts than Dick Tracy. She'd be a terror in the boardroom with her skill at the full frontal attack.

He scooped up the knife and snapped all the tools into their slots with one hand. "I must've left it here when I was putting on the switch plates. Thanks." He turned to Mallory. "Until I get that order, I can't do much more today. I'll see you around."

To her intense relief, he walked out as easily as he'd come in, and she heard his car start up and pull away. It took a few moments for her breathing to slow to its normal rate.

"That was one fine-looking man," Elaine commented with relish. "It's almost worth doing an addition to have someone like that around."

"And listen to Mom lecturing about how grungy he looks and smells and how awful it must be to live in a trailer on the poor side of town?"

Elaine looked rueful. "He doesn't smell, but you're

right. It ain't worth it." Elaine collected the scripts and her purse, and kissed Mallory goodbye. "It's been fun, sweetie. See you later."

"Bye." She closed the front door behind her and leaned on it. Breathe. In. Out. All clear. Too bad he'd taken the wretched knife with him before she'd used one of the attachments on him herself...and she'd take great pleasure in deciding which one.

On the heels of that thought, the man himself reappeared. He rapped on the door with his knuckles. "Is it safe?"

"No thanks to you. Is that what you call working undercover—leaving your stuff all over like a trail of crumbs?"

"Sorry about that. It won't happen again."

"You keep saying that. My sister is the most suspicious person on the planet. And you can bet my mom won't be far behind once she gets wind of you."

"Nothing wrong with that. I'm a contractor as far as anyone else knows."

Mallory shot him a look dark with warning. "You haven't met my mom."

He rolled up the sleeves of his dark gray Henley shirt, baring his forearms. His watch, she saw, was the kind divers and engineers wore to help them navigate through hostile territory, not to tell time.

"I didn't bring much. My bag and my camera. I'll put it in one of the unused rooms upstairs. It's not likely anyone will go in there, is it?"

Lord, he had nice hands. Men shouldn't be allowed

to expose their forearms like that, especially when they were nicely covered in hair.

Just right.

Get real. That man isn't about to expose any more for you at any time.

She shook her head in answer to his question and pushed the screen door open. After this debacle, she needed air, not paint fumes. She pulled on her gardening gloves, located an ancient trowel in the garage and walked out into the yard to inspect the riot of greenery the Realtor had called a garden.

Enchanted forest was right. She hated to agree with Elaine and her mother, but had she bitten off more than she could chew? Along with everything else, she had to put in some time on the yard, or she really would wind up like Sleeping Beauty, looking out at the world through a hedge that reached to the roof.

The sun felt warm on her back as she got into the rhythm of pulling and trimming, the scent of crushed leaves sweet in her nostrils. It was almost hypnotic. Peaceful. Like meditation.

Across the street, a car rolled to a stop at Blake's curb, and a middle-aged man got out. She was tempted to wave and tell him Blake was at work, but she felt too sun-warmed and lazy. The man pushed something through the unused cat door and then jogged back to his car and drove away.

A few minutes later, another car purred down the block and parked. Good grief. Didn't Blake's friends know that he had a day job, for goodness' sake?

Her sense of peace evaporated when she looked up to see Jon Easton standing on the path.

"Hello, Mallory," he said with a smile, and picked his way over a broken flagstone. He was dressed like a *GQ* model, his shirt and tie perfectly matched to the fine wool of his suit. His Bruno Maglis gleamed, having never actually touched the soil between the flat stones of the path. Jon took his sunglasses off and poked them into the inner pocket of his jacket. He never pushed them up into his hair like a normal person—that would spoil the lines of his latest ninety-dollar trim.

"This is a first." It didn't matter what her clothes looked like, she reminded herself, or what her hair was doing. She was working and proud of it. "What are you doing out on the street in the middle of the day?"

He smiled, and she wondered instantly what he was up to. "I had a meeting at headquarters this morning and gave up face time with the president so I could come by and see you."

"I'm honored. You shouldn't have."

"I want to talk. I was hoping to at your mom's the other night, but it seems you had another appointment."

She hated it when he loomed over her like that. Mallory got up, slapped the gloves together and dropped them on the pile of weeds. She leaned against a crepe myrtle, in the shade, and waited.

Jon looked from her to the grass she stood on. Grass grew in dirt. She could practically read his mind.

"I'd rather talk inside. I've got a full calendar this afternoon. I can't sit on the ground in this suit."

"I'm under construction inside. You know, Sheetrock dust. Varnish. Nails sticking out everywhere."

"Oh. In that case, out here's fine." The man she had once thought she loved squinted against the sun and looked the front of her house up and down. "Well, you must be working on the inside first."

"Yes, I am. The kitchen cabinets just came."

"Don't leave the outside too long. Look at all that rust." He pointed at one of the downspouts. "You should have it fixed now, while the weather's good." His tone was earnest, but it had been just as earnest when he had explained why the black patent slingbacks were vital to the meeting that final morning of their engagement.

"I know that, Jon."

"You should—"

"You know what?"

"What?" She could hear annoyance under the surface cordiality of his tone. He had been CEO of SpendSafe, and was now a senior vice president at the company that had bought them out. Jon Easton was not used to being interrupted.

"You're the only person I know who sees the world as it should be, not as it is. The problem is, no one but you knows what it should be, so no one can ever measure up."

"Mallory, you were a tech major, not a psych major. Can you please be fair?"

"It isn't psychology at all. It's simple science, based

on the observation of repeated events. In your case, repeated and repeated."

She watched him control himself and swallow what he obviously wanted to say. "I didn't come over to fight. I want us to be friends, if we can't be anything else. Your mother worries about you. I do, too."

"Why?"

"Isn't that obvious? You buy a house that was on the market for months because nobody else even wanted it for a teardown. You cash out your stock options and, instead of investing in Ocean Tech like a reasonable person would, you sink half the money into this and it still looks like—" He stopped, chose different words. "Like it did when you bought it. You cut yourself off from the people who love you. Yes, we're worried."

"You don't need to be," Mallory said gently. "And that money you're worried about is safely invested. I'm having fun. I'm happy. If those two things don't work for you, that's too bad. I can appreciate the results of my own work."

"You had all that at SpendSafe. You could still have it. The offer from Ocean Tech still holds, you know. You could be running their R&D group starting Monday, if you wanted."

She shook her head. "I'm meeting with the floor guys Monday. Sorry."

"Please be serious. I could hire you in a second."

"No. I don't need any more money. Voice-over jobs pay for the groceries. And truth be told, I kind of like telling contractors what to do. Maybe I should get my own license."

He looked at her closely and his jaw tightened. "I hope not. The software industry needs more minds like yours. You're wasted on this radio commercial thing. Every time I hear one, I cringe. And every time I see Lorne Andrews at the board meeting, I could choke him for getting you into it. You shouldn't let yourself be distracted by stuff like that. I need you on my team."

Somehow the words of praise didn't ring very true, coming from between his teeth like that. Jon didn't lead teams, anyway. He led parades. Not for the first time, she thanked heaven she'd seen it in time.

"I happen to like doing commercials. I do them for fun, Jon. *F-u-n.* And Lorne didn't get me into them. His job is marketing. He has a sense for what people like. He just made a suggestion about radio to the bank president, and I took it from there."

"I don't mean *team* in only a business sense. You know my feelings for you haven't changed."

"I can't, Jon. Everything's different now."

"What do you mean?" He made as if to step onto the lawn and her muscles tensed, but he retreated back to the solidity of the flagstones. "Is there someone else? A carpenter? Or somebody at this bank?"

Someone else in her life? It wouldn't hurt for him to think so. "That's hardly a fair question. Your relationships are none of *my* business. Give me the same courtesy."

"You know there isn't anyone else." He took a few

steps toward the glistening black BMW that blocked the end of her path. "But I'll respect your feelings for now. And I'll have my assistant send a contractor down to measure for new downspouts."

Mallory pushed away from the tree. "You will not. This is my home. I'll hire my own contractors. If you send one, I'll sic Kiko on him. Which reminds me, when are you going to take her?"

He climbed into the car and the passenger window slid down. He leaned across the seat. "I'm not in a position to care for an animal at the moment. I assume you're caring for her, right, not mistreating her in my memory?"

She would not give him the satisfaction of seeing her stamp her foot in the street, so she did it behind the screen of the crepe myrtle as he drove away. "Ooh!"

"Friend of yours?" drawled a voice above her.

She whirled and looked up. Duncan Moore leaned on the deck railing. The stubble shadowed his face, accentuating the planes of cheek and jaw. His hair was rumpled, as if he'd been raking his hands through it.

There you are, she fumed silently, *after everything is over.*

Her palms tingled. But whether it was because she wanted to slap someone, or touch someone, she couldn't tell.

"That was my ex-fiancé." In the street, the dust of Jon's departure drifted slowly back to earth. "He just said something really unfair."

"Ah. Not on friendly terms, I take it."

"That's none of your business." He raised an eyebrow. Well, let him. She could keep her mouth shut, too. She jerked on her gloves and started pulling the weeds again.

He loped down the stairs to join her. "So you got in on the SpendSafe IPO," he said. "I heard it went for ten or fifteen mil."

She glared at him. "Were you eavesdropping?"

"Not intentionally. The windows are open, and you guys weren't all that discreet." He glanced at her pile of weeds. "Can I give you some help out here?"

Her hand jerked and she dropped the trowel, then reached to pull a weed as if that was what she had meant to do. "I thought you were surveilling."

"I'm off duty at the moment."

She wasn't sure how someone decided they were off duty with this kind of a job. Maybe he'd reached his daily quota of license plate numbers.

"My yard is a disaster." Mallory dug a thistle out of the ground and tossed it on the growing pile of weeds beside her. "Jon's answer to everything is to hire someone to do it. But I'm not going to. Not until I know it's defeated me."

"I've never seen anybody work so hard. Did you do all that painting?"

"No. A guy who works on the houses my mom sells did most of it. Up until now I thought I could do the other stuff, but now I'm not so sure."

"Why would you want to?" He knelt beside her and began pulling chickweed. "There are plenty of people who'd be happy to do it for you."

"I don't want someone else to do it for me. This place is mine."

"Yeah, I figured that. A woman's downspouts are her own business. But your friend across the road seems willing to help."

"I try not to impose on my neighbors, and I certainly don't need Jon's staff to make calls for me. Besides, that's not the point." She jerked on a circle of dandelion leaves the size of a dinner plate. The root broke off, and she sucked a breath between her teeth. "Did you ever do paint-by-numbers when you were a kid?"

"Nope. I built model planes. Glue and balsa wood and tissue paper." He worked quickly. His pile was getting bigger than hers.

"I did them because I had no artistic talent. My sister would come along when I wasn't there and paint in pieces of the picture. She never stayed inside the lines and it used to drive me nuts. This house is my personal paint-by-numbers and nobody's going to mess with it."

"I'd say you have lots of artistic talent." He looked up at the wraparound porch and the riot of climbing roses that hung over the rail. "It's going to be a showpiece when you're done."

"You think so?"

"Yeah. I see what you mean about the paint-by-numbers. Bit by bit you fill in the spaces with floors and cabinets and stuff, and even though it doesn't make sense while it's happening, when it comes together you see how beautiful it is."

"Yes. That's it exactly." Her irritation faded and was replaced by a sense of discovery. "Most people would just say I was hopelessly anal." His gaze flicked up and caught hers, and for a moment recognition flashed between them. And something else.

"An orderly mind doesn't have to be anal." He broke eye contact and renewed his attack on the chickweed.

"You don't have to do this, you know." She hardly knew what she was saying, she was so shaken by that brief moment of accord.

"It's the least I can do."

Far be it from her to stop the man if he wanted to spend his time weeding. It felt...companionable. Strange. Something she could definitely get used to if—

Yeah, sure. Get a grip on those fantasies, woman. He's working off what he considers an obligation. Digging weeds does not equal making a pass.

He held out his hand for the trowel, and she handed it over as a nurse would give a scalpel to a surgeon. She couldn't remember the last time she'd worked so seamlessly with a man. Jon wasn't the gardening type—it was really hard on the knees of the Armani suits.

"What are the chances you'll have company again?"

"Depends on what's going on. My mom might come by. I haven't been able to train her to call first."

He looked up and raised an eyebrow. "I don't suppose she'd approve of you hiding investigators in the shrubbery."

"Are you eligible? Rich? Well dressed?" She knelt in the grass beside him and moved his pile out of the way so he could start on the next section of the border.

"No, on all counts."

"Then I'm afraid you're not going to make it onto her Christmas list."

He jabbed the trowel under a thistle and levered it up so hard that dirt flew. "Hers doesn't concern me so much."

He angled a penetrating glance at her, and again she felt that deep tremor of recognition. She used to laugh when Elaine would tell her about her friends' "eyes meeting across the room." All Mallory could imagine was flying eyeballs. Now she understood. There was something in Duncan's gaze that went through to her bones.

"I...um...it doesn't?"

His eyelashes were stubby and thick and blonde. Like his hair. Thick. Dark blond. She wanted to touch it. Him. She wanted to touch him.

"No," he whispered.

Beautiful mouth. Kiss me. Kiss me.

Their shoulders bumped. She smelled hot skin and mint, and a thrill of anticipation rocketed through her as her gaze locked with his across the few inches that separated them.

She closed the gap, swaying toward him until her lips touched his, the merest whisper of a kiss.

"Mallory," he breathed. His hands came up to her

shoulders, and equally gently, he set her away from him. "I can't do this."

She flushed with humiliation, hated the way her skin betrayed every emotion. "You're married, right?"

"No." He laughed. "Far from it."

"Then what? You have a thing against chubby, unemployed women?"

He stared at her, still holding her shoulders. "Chubby? Right, like the Venus de Milo is chubby. Or any other goddess you could name."

She pulled away and jabbed the trowel under a plant, slicing its young roots off with the sharp edge. "Don't make fun of me."

"I'm not. It's a matter of ethics." His voice was husky, as if he were having a hard time getting the right words out. "I can't involve you in an investigation."

She glanced at him over her shoulder, and almost against her will, her gaze dropped to his mouth. "I'm already aiding and abetting you. And the investigation didn't kiss me last night."

He swallowed. "I apologized for that. And promised it wouldn't happen again. I meant it."

"I don't see what watching for somebody's husband has to do with me."

"Wife. I can't tell you the details. But I don't make it a practice to get involved with people in my cases."

She wished she'd left it alone. Now he made it sound as if she was one of many faceless women, all throwing themselves at him, refusing to leave when he asked.

"But you're in my room. I'm already involved."

"Yes, but it isn't personal."

No, it wasn't. That had been Jon's problem, too. He had wanted her for her business acumen and her technical knowledge. He'd wanted her on his arm at venture capital parties. But when it came to a relationship, deep down, he hadn't been able to connect on the most personal level.

She was doomed to attract men who didn't want to get personal but didn't want to leave.

Great. Well, she knew someone who did want to get personal. Maybe she should reconsider her feelings on that point.

"You're right, it's not," she said. She got up and dusted soil off the front of her skirt. "If you'll excuse me, I've got to go make a phone call. Nothing personal, but my girlfriend Carly and I are going out Friday night. I think I'll see if Blake wants to go along."

5

IN THE PAST COUPLE of days he'd kicked himself so many times, his psyche had bruises.

Duncan's body had been at war with his brain in a way that hadn't happened in years. So he was attracted to Mallory Baines. That wasn't the problem. He could deal with that. The problem was, he was beginning to like her. He liked the way her spunk showed through her nice-girl upbringing. He liked her dedication to her goals. And he really liked looking at her.

He hated to think she would know anything about what Blake Purdue was up to, but if she were dating him it was possible. And thanks to Duncan's misguided chivalry in the garden yesterday, it definitely looked like she was dating him.

The investigator in him liked that. The more they were together, the more likely it was that she might let something slip.

But the man who had kissed her hated it. He hated that he didn't know her well enough to judge her character. He hated that his body came to attention the minute she walked into a room. Most of all, he hated how his mind wouldn't let him do what he wanted to do, which was grab her and kiss her senseless.

How had he gotten himself into this?

Beside him, Geoff drained his beer and signaled to the cocktail waitress, who was dressed in something that approximated a cancan girl's outfit. The abbreviated ruffly skirts didn't conceal much. Onstage in the Lucky Miner's ballroom, the band was doing a competent job of "Texas Rain." He and Geoff had a small gilded table off to the side so they could see both entrances, but be hidden by some plants. Some habits never wore off.

Duncan had tailed Mallory here and met Geoff at one of the side doors of the Lucky Miner, where—what a coincidence—Twenty-First Century had the security contract. A casino wasn't one of his favorite places in the world, but there was no way he was going to let Mallory or Purdue out of his sight tonight.

"Hey." Geoff nudged him. "I've got the eye. Check out the brunette sitting down at their table."

Ever the optimist—despite his two divorces. The woman he indicated wore a strapless red piece of engineering that was enough to make a man's eyes pop. But Duncan had seen her already, when Mallory had stopped to pick her up. Mallory was the one he was concerned about. She was wearing a little black dress that did amazing things to her curves. And next to her was the prince of darkness himself.

"She's a friend of the woman who owns my surveillance post. But we're not looking at her. We're looking at him. Seen him before?"

"No. And believe me, we've got so many companies losing parts I know all the usual suspects by sight. Know the brunette's name?"

Duncan raised an eyebrow. "Carla. Cathy. Something like that. Since when did you start robbing the cradle?"

"Since my last divorce went through. I figure I've got to catch one young and train her properly."

"That ought to appeal to her." Duncan tasted his beer. "You can't afford her, anyway."

"I know. I can't afford myself right now. Maybe she'd settle for a drink."

"I've got a problem here, and you're not helping," Duncan complained. "Focus."

"I am," Geoff protested. "My eyes haven't left their table since they sat down."

Screened by the crowd in the ballroom, some of whom were already dancing, Duncan watched Mallory's body language. She sat in profile to him, Purdue on her left. The other girl—Carly, that was her name—sat on Purdue's other side. One moment Mallory would smile and tilt her head close to Purdue to listen to what he said, the next she'd sit back as if her resources had been temporarily expended. Her smile faded slightly at the corners, and she glanced over the crowd as if she'd come to the prom with the wrong guy and was still hoping her dream date would show up. One foot in a high-heeled shoe tapped to the four-four beat.

Duncan leaned toward Geoff. "You ever hear anything about this place?"

Geoff didn't need to be told what he meant. "Yup. No proof."

"Like what?"

"Like maybe a bit of backroom gambling might be going on. And some blackmail to go with it. You may have noticed a smaller than usual number of my people here. The management pays well, but I'm not so sure they're completely committed to security. I would hate to think I was a token rent-a-cop, but nothing else explains it."

Interesting.

The band swung into a faster number. Half the crowd leaped to their feet. Blake leaned over to Mallory and said something, and she shook her head with a smile, tapping her empty glass. He started to get up, but she waved him back down and began to make her way over to the bar.

"Keep an eye on him," he told Geoff. "I'll be right back."

He circled around the rear of the room to the bar. When the casino had opened, the paper had reported that the bar itself had come from a real Old West saloon somewhere in Nevada, but he doubted it. It was too big and too glossy. Money had been spent with a free hand, and the owners were making it back in spades.

He wondered how much of the profit was legal.

"Oops. Sorry, miss."

Mallory steadied her replenished wineglass and turned with an absent social smile. Then her eyes widened. He hoped his look of surprise was as genuine.

"What are you doing here?" she exclaimed.

He nodded toward the stage. "I heard they'd be playing tonight. A friend of mine likes them. You?"

She looked uncomfortable and glanced past him at her table. "I, um...me, too."

She was a pretty good liar. Not quite as good as he was, but close. The music segued into a slow dance number and he had an idea. This might just be a date. Then again, it might not. Blake had to unload the parts somewhere. If the casino's reputation wasn't exactly sterling, there was a good possibility he might have a connection here. Now would be a fine time to find out.

"Like to dance?"

She hesitated, then lifted her glass. "I just got this. I should really—"

"Take it to your table. I'll wait."

"But I just told..." Her voice trailed off, then she looked at Purdue and seemed to make up her mind. "I'd love to. I'll be back in a sec."

Reflected light slid along the lines of her dress at hip and thigh as she wound between the tables. He didn't know what kind of fabric it was, but it clung to her as if it were a second skin.

He shook himself. *Focus.* What was he going to do once he got her out on the dance floor? Apologize? Interrogate her? Apologize, then interrogate?

He couldn't come right out and say, "Are you sleeping with the guy or not? And if you are, got any interesting pillow talk you'd like to pass along?" The best he could hope for was a casual comment, a passing hint that she might know something.

Duncan hardly ever got to build a case with whole bricks. He was used to making do with bits of rubble, piecing them together as if he were an archaeologist reconstructing a lost civilization. But with enough pieces, he could see the patterns, figure out the truth.

One thing was certain: If she were dancing with him, she wouldn't be dancing with Blake Purdue.

She joined him on the dance floor with a smile. He took her hand and slid his left arm around her waist. The fabric was hot at the small of her back. She moved closer, and he breathed in the fragrance of her hair. After a moment their bodies found the rhythm of the music, and he settled her against him.

He hadn't felt anything so good in years. Her thighs moved with his as he guided her in a slow circuit of the dance floor. He hardly knew what his feet were doing. The rest of him was shouting hallelujah at the sweet pressure of her breasts against his chest and the way the spotlights overhead gleamed on the smooth skin of her bare shoulders and glittered in her eyes.

He felt himself stiffen, and he came back to earth with a jolt. *Get your mind back on business before she has you arrested.*

"I'm sorry I upset you yesterday," he said gruffly.

She stirred, as though she were waking from a spell. "It was nothing personal."

Was she being serious or sarcastic? "Right," he said. "Just like this dance is nothing personal."

He gathered her a little closer, in case she decided to cut and run. The top of her head tucked neatly under his chin. "I wouldn't go that far."

"You're a good dancer. What I'd like to know is why you asked me."

Because I'm trying to keep you away from my suspect. "So I could apologize without risking a glass of wine in the face?"

"Nice try." The odd, detached tone began to leak out of her voice. "Really. Why?"

Duncan reached past the surface truth to the one beneath it. "Because you're beautiful and I wanted to."

"Ha-ha, funny guy. Wait till we get back to my table. I have a glass of wine with your name on it."

He spoke into her ear. "Because what I said about ethics is true. Because a dance is all I'm entitled to."

"And how do you know that?" She turned her head, and her breath fell warm on the side of his neck with each word. Again his treacherous body tightened.

"Because you're here with your neighbor. I got the message pretty clearly that you were off-limits as far as he was concerned. And that's okay. I just hope he's a nice guy who treats you like you deserve."

"No, you've got it—"

A large, tweedy, familiar shoulder brushed him and he turned, instinctively pulling Mallory a little closer.

"Hey, *mija*," Carly said to Mallory as she swayed past, her arms looped around Geoff's neck.

What the—? So much for trusting his backup. Duncan shot a poisonous glare at Geoff and looked around wildly.

All three chairs at Mallory's table were empty.

Instinct leaped to battle with desire. His body definitely did not want to go chase Blake Purdue. Both his arms had abandoned the dance hold and somehow found their way around Mallory's waist. But his mind clicked through possibilities at ninety miles an hour. Purdue was not dancing. He wasn't at the bar. He wasn't listening to the band.

So where was he, and why had he given two beautiful women the slip at the first opportunity?

Anomalies. Something was up.

The problem was, his target could be anywhere in this casino, billed as one of the largest outside Nevada. Where could he start the search? And how could he do it without dumping Mallory flat and putting his surveillance post in jeopardy?

This was what he got for listening to his body in the first place, dammit. He should have just stayed in the background and discreetly tailed Purdue into the casino's dark corners, listening from behind the red velvet draperies. If there was a jackpot waiting out there for this case, he had just put it at risk.

The band finished the slow number and shifted back into a faster gear. Mallory pulled away.

"I think I'm ready for my wine," she said. Her voice was soft, almost dreamy.

His body responded to a tone that should only be used in the bedroom, and he cursed his inability to keep his mind on business. The fact was, he didn't want to leave her. But he couldn't sit at a table while Purdue was at large and getting into mischief.

"I've heard this place is a real showpiece," he said. They reached her table and he handed her the untouched glass. "Feel like walking around and having a look?"

She glanced out at the dance floor, but neither Geoff nor Carly was in sight. "Sure."

They strolled through gambling areas done up like the heyday of the Gold Rush. Dice clicked, roulette wheels clattered, and music drifted out of speakers hidden in the gilded heads of cupids.

Duncan's senses warred between the urge to slide an arm around Mallory's bare shoulders, or at the very least take her hand, and the need to keep his distance until he knew what was going on.

He just hadn't expected it to be this difficult.

The place was as huge inside as it had looked from the parking lot. He was never going to find Purdue. Any minute now Mallory was going to lose interest in yet another blackjack salon and insist on getting her money's worth out of her concert ticket.

His instincts were probably wrong, anyway. The guy had probably just gotten bored sitting at the table alone, and decided to shoot a few games of craps while he waited for the girls to come back.

"Danny!" Mallory exclaimed suddenly. She waved at someone on the far side of the salon they'd just entered, and tugged on Duncan's arm. "That's a friend of mine, over there with Blake. I'm going to say hi."

Ka-ching! Life was a row of cherries.

A deeply tanned man in his late twenties stood as Mallory came up to their table. "Mallory. How good to see you." He nodded his head, then looked surprised as she hugged him.

"I'm not your manager anymore, Danny. Duncan, this is Danny Barda. We started out in product development together, before Jon and I started SpendSafe."

Danny was as thin as a piece of kelp, with the same sense of strong resilience despite the stoop to his shoulders. Duncan shook hands with him and then with Purdue, who was looking from Duncan to Mallory with undisguised curiosity.

"Aren't you the contractor?" he asked. "What are you doing here?"

Mallory overrode him in her delight at seeing an old friend. "Danny, how are you? And your sister? I heard Hope was getting married."

"Yes," he said softly. "She is married. I heard you were, too, to the big boss."

"That was a malicious rumor," she said with a grin. "No marriage for me, thanks. I'm too busy fixing up my house. What a coincidence you know Blake. We live across the street from each other."

Danny shrugged. "It's this valley. Everybody gets to know everybody in the computer business. Did you know Hope and I are both at SiliconNext?"

Duncan looked sharply at the young man. His client's company. And he was meeting Blake Purdue under fishy circumstances. Duncan's instincts had been dead on target.

"Lucky you," Mallory replied. "I knew Barbara Mashita when we were both working the venture capital parties. She's much better at it than I am. And a way better dresser."

"She's a good boss." Danny seemed uncomfortable.

"Well, I should go find the rest of my party. Nice to have run into you, Blake, Mallory."

Duncan watched him leave the salon and wondered what had made him slide out from under the conversation the moment Barbara's name had come up. Was he feeling a little guilty at defrauding an employer he obviously liked? Or was he just shy?

Duncan had a feeling it wasn't the latter.

6

THE LUCKY MINER WAS the only one who seemed to be getting lucky, Mallory thought. She watched Danny leave and wondered if it would be too rude to ask Duncan to go back to the ballroom so they could dance. Dancing with Duncan, in her opinion, was the next best thing to sex, and if she hadn't been mistaken, his body thought so, too.

Putting the feelings of others before her own had been drummed into her since childhood. Not that it was a bad rule to live by. But in her family, it seemed as though she was always the one making concessions, always the one giving up what she wanted to make other people happy. When Blake had asked her to dance, it had taken some real spine to turn him down. After all, asking him to be part of a threesome wasn't the same as being his date. No matter how piqued she'd been after the incident in the garden, no matter how much she wanted her feelings to change, she just couldn't do it.

But good girls got their reward, even when they were bad. She'd danced with Duncan, and right now she wanted to do it again—as soon as possible.

"I'm going back to the ballroom, guys," she said. Could Duncan take a hint?

"I'll go with you." Blake put his empty glass on a nearby table. "The first set is probably over, though."

"Shame to miss it," Duncan agreed. "But if you'd rather play another game, I can take Mallory to her table."

"That's okay." Blake's smile was smooth, his blue eyes friendly. He was a living definition of the boy next door as he began to walk with them back to the ballroom. "Are you ready to dance with me yet, Mallory?"

He no longer reminded her of a golden retriever. More like one of those mastiffs with the big paws and the smiley teeth. But he was her neighbor. He'd spent many of his Saturday afternoons getting paint spatters on his jeans for her sake, and all he asked for, in return, was a dance.

She could do that. Payment in full. One dance.

"Sure," she agreed. He took her hand and spun her into his arms. She narrowly missed getting a case of whiplash, since she'd been looking back at Duncan at the time, watching him settle his rangy body on one of the spindly gold chairs.

Blake wasn't a bad dancer. His only fault was that he wasn't Duncan. She shouldn't hold that against him. He was trying so hard to narrow the gap between them that she gave up and relaxed, allowing him to pull her snugly against his chest.

Payback really sucked.

When the band finally, blessedly, wound up the song, Carly and her partner, a big blond bear of a guy in his early forties, arrived back at the table at the same time she and Blake did.

"Hey, Mal," Carly said breathlessly over the applause. "What's happening? Ready to go?"

"Go? We just got here."

"It's a one-set show. They've been playing for almost an hour. That was their third encore."

And she'd missed all but two dances because she'd been wandering around in a daze, wishing Duncan would touch her. Which it didn't seem likely he was going to do. Not tonight, at any rate. He just sat at the table with a distracted look on his face.

"If you want, Carly, I'll take you home," the blond man offered.

Alarmed, Mallory shot a glance at her friend. *Is that okay?* she asked silently with a quick lift of her eyebrows. *More to the point, is he?*

Definitely okay. Carly's nod was firm on that point. *Catch you up later.*

The blond man took Carly's hand and they left without another word, the air practically sizzling in their wake.

"Thanks a lot, Geoff," Duncan muttered.

"You know him?" she asked.

"Yeah, he's a friend."

"How good a friend?" She was starting to sound like her own mother. Carly was a big girl. But....

"I've known him for years. Trust me. Your friend is safe with him."

Great. She, on the other hand, faced the happy prospect of driving home forty miles with Blake. No Duncan. No dancing. Unless—

She turned to him. "Did you bring your own car or—"

He cut her off by grabbing her around the waist and whirling her out onto the dance floor. It was practically empty, the only music piped in from the house speakers.

"What are you doing?" she protested. She tried to push him away, but he kept his arms stiff, holding her in place against him.

"What are *you* doing? Yeah, I drove, but I can't follow you home. No one is supposed to know I'm there, right?"

"Oh." She'd completely forgotten he was a private detective, that he was only using her bedroom for business purposes. She had no idea what he and his friend were doing here, but it probably wasn't to listen to the band. There was probably some extortion thing going on, or an unfaithful husband behind the potted palms. He was only dancing with her now to get her out of earshot. Their previous dance had probably been a cover-up for eavesdropping, and she'd been so caught up in enjoying him she'd just assumed he was feeling the same way.

"When are you coming back?"

"That's not your problem."

Imagination was her problem. She must have been hallucinating when she'd thought there was something special about their dance. Private detectives were the next best thing to law enforcement, right? A dance with her probably ranked right up there with helping little old ladies across the street and rescuing cats from trees.

NEXT TIME DUNCAN TALKED to Geoff, he was going to get an earful he wouldn't forget. It was sheer luck that Mallory had recognized Danny and led him to Blake. They both should have been quietly tailing him, identifying players, watching connections. Working.

Not coming on to the suspect's known associates.

Duncan tailed Mallory's very late-model European sports car at a discreet distance back to Santa Rita.

When they pulled over in front of Purdue's house, Duncan stopped half a block away to watch. Purdue's silhouette leaned toward Mallory's, and Duncan craned forward. Was he trying a friendly kiss goodnight? Or asking for a date that wasn't a threesome?

Duncan couldn't see or hear anything. And why should he care?

Dumb question. He cared. If Mallory kissed Purdue it would change every detail of the case.

Purdue got out of her car and watched Mallory pull into her driveway, then turned slowly and went into his house. Duncan left his car where it was and jogged down to the beach, approaching her house from the side with no criminals on it. The back door was open, so he let himself in silently and mounted the stairs to his surveillance post.

He pushed the door open, and she shrieked and dropped her wrap. She flattened herself against the closet door and glared at him, one hand pressed below her collarbone.

"What are you doing?" she managed between breaths.

"What's the matter? Got a guilty conscience?" He tried not to watch the rise and fall of her breasts under the soft black drape of her bodice, and failed miserably.

"Of course not," she snapped. "You scared me to death."

"You left the back door open," he pointed out reasonably.

"An oversight on my part." She picked up her wrap and hung it up. "Not only does Carly cut out on me, you do, too."

She slipped off her shoes, first one foot and then the other, hopping to keep her balance, and it was all he could do not to go down on his knees and offer to help.

"I told you why I had to. Besides, you had company for the ride home." Now he'd hear about the kiss, if there'd been one.

She wiggled her toes on the rug. "I love those shoes, but I hate driving in them."

"They looked nice." Understatement of the year. They made her legs about a mile long. Or maybe it was the way the hem of her dress flirted with her thighs that did that. Was she going to take the dress off in front of him, too?

Had Purdue kissed her, or not? And what had they talked about during that forty-minute drive home?

She put the shoes in the box they'd come in and reached up to put them on a shelf in the closet. He tried not to watch, but her hem slid up and gave him a flash of lace. His blood began a dark, heavy drumbeat in his groin. She was wearing lace-topped stockings, not panty hose.

He needed to get out of this room.

But he also needed to hear what she had to say about Purdue. He had to control his rioting senses. Stay rational. Do the right thing. No matter what it cost him.

She stopped by the window and looked out over the darkened street. "How funny," she said in a voice that meant something was odd, not comical.

He still hadn't recovered from the lace or her reticence about Purdue. "What?"

Look away from this woman and go downstairs.

"Blake's got company."

Her words hit him with all the force of a cold shower. He pushed away from the door and joined her at the window in two strides.

A four-door import rolled to a stop at Blake's curb, and a woman got out. She was tiny, not much more than five-four, and her hair was bundled up at the back of her neck. She pulled off her white lab coat and tossed it in the back seat, but not before she'd removed a small package and tucked it into the pocket of her skirt.

Where was his camera when he needed it? Behind him, on the floor. No time to grab it. He cursed and beside him, Mallory jumped.

"I don't get it," she said. "What's Hope doing?"

The woman slipped through Purdue's back door and Duncan turned to stare at Mallory. "You know that girl?"

"Yes. It's Danny's sister. You know, Danny, the man we ran into at the casino." She paused for a moment. "Oh, no. That's not your cheating wife, is it?"

He thought fast. Once again, he had no idea how close she was to any of these people. If he said yes, she could pick up the phone, call Hope, and verify he was wrong. On the other hand, if he said no, he'd have no reason to get the camera and do what he needed to do.

The woman reappeared.

"Yeah, I'm afraid that's who it is." He grabbed the camera from the floor behind the chair, and squeezed off a couple of shots as she got into her car. When she drove off, he snapped the lens cap back on and prepared to lie.

Mallory regarded him for a moment and shook her head. "I don't believe it."

He shrugged one shoulder toward the window. "There's your proof. Maybe the marriage didn't work out."

"I know the man she married. He used to work for me."

"Everyone used to work for you, it seems."

"Like Danny said, it's the Valley. Hope would not cheat on John LaCrosse. Besides, she wasn't even in there long enough to say hello, much less—" She stopped.

"Much less what?"

"Do anything else."

This was not good. He wasn't prepared, didn't have a story ready to give her. Drastic action had to happen here, and fast. For once he decided to go with his gut instead of his brain.

"Like what, Mallory? Like maybe something you'd like to do?"

"What?" Blank surprise blotted out the defensive tone in her voice. "Did I just miss something?"

He'd meant to disorient her, and he'd succeeded. He sat beside her on the bed. She edged away. In another second she'd jump up and run.

"Do you wish it were you?" he asked softly. "With Blake?"

She stopped edging and turned to face him. "Are you nuts?"

The hem of her dress slid up. Resolutely he ignored it. He was going to get to the bottom of this if it killed him.

"We got interrupted back at the casino. Just when you were going to tell me how it stands with you and Blake."

"It? What it? There is no *it* with Blake and me. The man is my neighbor. That's all."

"Your neighbor who helps you with the painting. Who protects you from strange men. Who has joint custody of your cat. Come on, Mallory."

Somehow he'd managed to lean in until his mouth was six inches from hers. Their knees were almost touching, and if he moved his finger he could touch the filmy skirt that rode up another fraction every time she moved.

"Why is it so important to you who my friends are?" Her voice sounded a little thready.

"Is that all he is? A friend? Nothing more?"

"Would it bother you if he was?"

He closed the gap. "Answer the question." He'd meant to scare her off the subject of Hope, make her train of thought jump its track, but the clean scent of her skin and the warm fragrance of her shampoo ambushed him. In one brief second, the train of his own thoughts hit the switch and swerved.

"What question?" she whispered.

He leaned in and breathed. "You smell good." His blood was doing a jungle dance in his veins now.

"If you want me to talk about my friends, you should just say so." Her voice had gone from thready to breathless. But she hadn't run yet.

"I don't want to talk at all," he murmured against the soft skin of her neck. He gave up trying to fool himself. At this moment, with common sense draining out of his brain and his body on fire, he could no longer think about Blake Purdue. This was what he'd wanted from the moment she'd opened the front door and rocked him back on his heels.

Gently he touched her skin with his lips, next to the skinny little spaghetti strap over her shoulder. She made an inarticulate sound, and his good intentions fizzled into nonexistence under the heat of the chase. The streetlight outside cast her in sharp silver-and-black relief, but his eyes had adjusted to the dark hours ago. He nuzzled her neck, and he could clearly see the generous outline of her breasts. Even as he watched, her nipples changed shape and hardened. First, black lace stockings. And now, no bra.

With momentous self-control, he touched her earlobe with the tip of his tongue. She shivered, and in reply, relaxed against him. His blood leaped in response.

Gently he kissed the soft spot under her ear, then turned her chin up, kissing a path along her jaw, her cheek, until finally her lips were an inch from his and the pounding in his body reached a fever pitch. He'd explode if he couldn't taste her.

"Yes," she breathed, and on the word he took her mouth. Those soft, full lips that had been making him crazy for days parted under his, and he changed angle, pulling her against his chest. She opened her mouth wider and her tongue found his in shy welcome.

"Mmm," someone said. He thought it might be himself, but by then it didn't matter. He teased her tongue with his, advancing, retreating, stroking in a sexual dance that was a preview of what might happen. What would happen if one of them didn't stop.

She broke the kiss and gasped for air. "This is crazy," she whispered. "We don't even know each other."

He tried to focus on her words. "I know a lot about you. I know you're smart." He pressed his lips to her throat. Her skin was so soft. "I know you like flowers. And kissing."

Somehow in the dark her mouth found his again, and he lost himself in the sweetness of it. She wound both arms around his neck, pulling his head down, urging him to kiss her harder. She moaned with pleasure, a tiny sound deep in her throat that inflamed him. He now knew one more thing about her. She wanted him in the same way he wanted her.

Pleasure and desire whipped through his veins at double speed. His palms ached for her skin, found one soft thigh below the hem of her dress. He groaned. Silky smooth. Hot. She murmured something into his hair.

"What was that?" he whispered. He rubbed his cheek on the soft fabric of her bodice. The heat of her firm flesh underneath inflamed him.

"Nothing," she sighed. "Kiss me."

But it had been something. The words took shape in his mind. "I'm not Blake?" He pulled back a little, trying to see her eyes in the gloom. They glittered in the silvery light from the street. "What?"

"That wasn't what I meant."

The rush of desire slowed and settled in his bones, as cold as disillusionment. As harsh as rejection. "Tell me."

"I didn't say anything." She wriggled away and cool air rushed between them.

Frustration collided with confusion. What the hell was she up to? And what was the matter with him? He'd blown a perfect chance to get some information out of her because he'd lost control.

Again.

Losing control led to failure. And if there was one thing he couldn't endure, it was the prospect of failing once more.

He stalked downstairs for the shower he should have taken ten minutes ago. Kiss or no kiss, she was a known associate of his suspect, and she didn't even have the sense to deny it. He could overcome this weakness that short-circuited his brain whenever she got within two feet of him. He could control his desire and keep his body under restraint.

Just watch him.

7

THE SHEETS WERE COLD and held no welcome. It took long moments before Mallory could get warm, long moments in which to think about what she'd done. What had possessed her to fall into the arms of a man who was practically a stranger? Was she so starved for affection that she'd disregard her own good sense?

There was no arguing with the pleasure part. Duncan Moore was not only a great dancer, he was some kisser, too. Somehow he had known how to touch her, to use his lips and his words to seduce her. And he'd done a better job of it in those few moments than Jon ever had in the years she'd known him.

But it had still been a mistake to let him know what she'd been thinking—that making love with the man who was wrong for her, but who was her own choice, rather than the men everyone else thought were right for her, would somehow set her free, the final step into her delayed adulthood. But she'd awakened from the haze of desire when he'd pulled back and shown her exactly what he thought of that idea.

Okay, so maybe it hadn't been very rational. Maybe it smacked a little of using him. But it hadn't felt as if she was using him. It had felt glorious. And now she'd never get another chance.

Mallory fell into an uneasy sleep, busy with dreams where she was chased by faceless men carrying handcuffs.

When the doorbell rang, she jerked awake as if she'd been shot. What time was it? She snatched the alarm off the night table and gasped. Ten o'clock in the morning!

The doorbell pealed again, and she rolled out of bed. She grabbed her jeans and yanked them on, and, with no time for a bra, pulled a sweatshirt over her head as she stumbled into the hallway and practically fell down the stairs.

Sounds of showering and a thin cloud of steam emanated from the bathroom. Oh, dear. Whoever it was, she'd have to chase them off until Duncan had shut himself in her room. If she was lucky, she wouldn't have to see him at all.

She opened the door and scanned the porch and yard. There was no one there.

In the bathroom, the shower shut off and the curtain rings clinked as he slid them back. Steam puffed into the hallway.

"Mallory!" her mother sang, stepping through the back door and into the kitchen. "Are you home?"

Mallory's heart jumped violently in her chest and she dashed down the hall.

Too late.

"Good morning, darling." Dorothy Baines smiled and leaned in for a kiss.

"Mom." She embraced her mother, careful not to crush Dorothy's lime green linen sheath. Only sixteen-year-olds should wear that shade, not respectable matrons of fifty-two. Even if it did look great on her. "New dress? That's some color."

"Thank you. It's the latest thing. They call it 'sorbet' and you put lavender accessories with it. A Realtor needs to look successful, or she'll never get any clients." She paused, looking Mallory up and down. "They have it in your size up at Neiman Marcus. You could put in a little time at the gym and then treat yourself."

"I'm not driving a hundred miles to San Francisco to buy a dress. Besides, in lime green I wouldn't look like the latest thing. I'd look like something that should be laid out at the morgue."

Her mother wrinkled her nose, but only a little. Making faces created wrinkles. "Such a way with words. I only meant that you should get some new things." She lifted an eyebrow at Mallory's sweatshirt, and Mallory stiffened. She would not wilt under the eyebrow. She would not.

"What if someone should happen to come over? Jon, for instance. Would you want him to see you like this?"

"He came already. He went away."

"I'm not surprised, when you treat him so badly."

"I was very nice to him, considering." She paused. Was there movement in the bathroom? "I don't want to talk about him, anyway." How much could Duncan hear?

"Why not? He talks about you very comfortably. We had a nice long visit after you walked out of my dinner party last week. Honestly, I brought you up to have better manners."

"Would you like some coffee, Mom?"

"Don't change the subject."

"I wasn't. I was just offering."

"No, thank you, dear. I was so humiliated."

"How do you think I felt? I don't know why you don't understand our relationship is over. Jon and I do not exist as a couple anymore."

"I don't understand why being with him was so horrible. He's well-off, he's handsome, he was good to you, he gave you this house, although that probably wasn't the wisest—"

"Excuse me, I paid for this house."

"But without cashing in your SpendSafe stock you wouldn't have had the means. He wants you back, Mallory. He told me so himself."

Was it her fate to be wanted by men she couldn't stand, when the one man she wanted kissed her like a lover and then treated her like a motel clerk?

"He doesn't want me, Mom. He wants the *idea* of me."

"I don't know what you mean." Her mother was beginning to get nettled, but Mallory couldn't seem to stop herself.

"That's okay, he doesn't, either. He has no idea about independence or even freedom of choice. But they come with the package now."

"You sound like a political commercial. Loving someone isn't about independence. Just the opposite."

Mallory sighed. They'd been having this same conversation for six months, and her mother was no closer to understanding than she had been when Mallory had arrived on her doorstep that first night, suitcase and determination firmly in hand.

"Mom, it's my life, good or bad. Having you go to bat for Jon doesn't help. It only makes me feel uncomfortable when I see him."

"That's a good sign. It means you still feel something."

"A healthy sense of relief."

"Oh, for heaven's sake. You're overreacting, just like Elaine."

Mallory swallowed. "Elaine?"

"I swear, something is up with that girl. I tried to have a visit with her yesterday between showings, and she was almost rude. She said she was working and didn't have time."

"She is working. She wants to get back into journalism."

"She doesn't have to work," her mother snapped. "Matt is a C.P.A. He takes good care of them."

"Sometimes you don't work because you have to. You work because you want to. To have something you've done that's just yours."

"And deprive some poor soul of a living, like you're doing with this silly radio thing?"

"Mom, that isn't even logical. The best candidate wins, whether she needs the job or not."

"I think it's perfectly logical and truthful. If she can stay at home, she should. Heaven knows my grandchildren shouldn't be latchkey children."

Uh-oh. Here it comes. Mallory braced herself.

"At least your children won't have to worry about a working mother." Dorothy paused. "When you finally meet someone and have them."

"Mom, don't even go there."

"If you're not going to reconcile with Jon, tell me how many men you've met lately. Eligible men. Not people covered in sweat and sawdust."

"A couple. And there's nothing wrong with dating a contractor. I'd rather have somebody who knew his way around a hammer than someone who screams every time his suit gets a spot on it."

"Have any of them asked you out?" Dorothy looked as though she didn't want to know the answer.

"No, of course not. Nor have I asked them."

"There you are. If you don't see people, you don't get to know them, you don't fall in love, you don't get married. Ten years from now you'll wake up in the middle of the night with a hot flash and it will be too late."

Hot flashes? She absolutely would not be caught having a conversation about hot flashes. The silence behind the bathroom door was getting on her nerves.

"So did you have something in mind when you came over, Mom?" she asked.

What was she thinking? Silence from the bathroom was a good thing. If he had any sense, Duncan would keep quiet until the coast was clear. She got the coffee beans out and ground them loudly until they were practically dust.

"I came over to ask you to—" Dorothy broke off

and stared at the bathroom door. A shaver had begun to hum behind it like a cheerful bumblebee. "Mallory."

Oh, dear. For a private detective, that man was a little short on sense. Now she was in for it. "Yes?"

"Who is in there?"

"Um, a friend." Please let him keep quiet, she prayed. Maybe she'll think it's Carly, doing her legs or something.

Under the sound of the shaver a male tenor hummed a bar of bluesy music. Dorothy grabbed her arm. "Mallory Elizabeth Baines, that is a man!"

"Yes, I know. Mom, that hurts. Let go."

"I will not let go until you tell me who it is."

"I did tell you. It's a friend."

Dorothy's eyes narrowed. "What kind of a friend?" Her laser gaze raked her daughter up and down, looking for evidence. "You haven't even brushed your hair yet. It's after ten on a Saturday morning and you just got out of bed!"

"It was a bit of a long night."

Dorothy threw Mallory's wrist away from her as if it might give her a disease. "Don't be crude with me, young lady."

"I only meant—"

"I see now why you and Elaine have been so secretive lately. And why you've been so abominably rude to Jon. It's because you've been with another man." Dorothy glared at her. "The least you could have done is told me before I embarrassed myself trying to mend the breach between you."

"I never asked you to mend any breaches. I told you before that my relationship—or not—with Jon was my business."

"I was only trying to help. And see what I get. I suppose the two of you were snickering all the time behind my back."

"No, not at all. And we aren't—"

"Oh, for heaven's sake. Give me credit for some intelligence."

Down the short hallway, the bathroom door opened and Duncan stepped out, his skin glowing from the hot water, a bath towel slung low around his hips.

Mallory's knees went weak, from the sight of all that skin, and the thought of what she'd done last night, and what her mother might do now.

A smile spread across his face. He gripped his towel with his left hand and held the other out as he walked up the hallway and into the kitchen. "You must be Mallory's mother. I'm Duncan Moore. Mallory's told me so much about you."

Dorothy's mouth opened, but no sound came out. Her social skills on automatic, she extended her hand and allowed Duncan to shake it. Her jaw snapped shut, and Mallory saw the muscles tighten. No doubt a flood of words was dammed up behind those clenched teeth.

"Dorothy Baines," her mother said finally. "It's a very great shame she didn't give me the same courtesy."

Mallory tried to catch Duncan's attention, and when that didn't work, she focused her concentration between his eyebrows. *Say you're a contractor,* she thought at him. *Say you're just borrowing the bathroom because you were here working late. Say you have a wife and five kids.*

Duncan shrugged, grin still in place. "Oh, that was my fault. I asked her to keep it secret. It's not often a man finds a treasure like Mallory. I wanted to keep her to myself as long as I could."

He turned a look on her so adoring that her mother blinked. The blood drained out of Mallory's head, leaving her with a distinct floating sensation.

"But now that we've met, I hope we'll get to be friends."

Keep what a secret? Keep her to himself? What was he doing?

"Yes," Dorothy said faintly. "Perhaps you might consider putting some clothes on, too."

He laughed. "Right. I was just so eager to meet you I completely forgot about the niceties. I'll be right back."

Dorothy watched Duncan and his towel disappear up the staircase. Mallory hesitated, torn between dashing up the stairs and screaming at him, and staying put to try to do damage control.

"Well. This has to be a first." Her mother took off her sorbet jacket as if she meant business.

Mallory swallowed and wished her knees didn't feel so rubbery. She was an adult, for heaven's sake. There had to be worse things than being caught practically flagrante delicto.

Or maybe not.

"So." Dorothy laid her handbag and the jacket on the counter. "Where did you meet this—what was his name?"

"Duncan Moore." What could she say that might sound remotely like the truth? "I—he was doing a little work around here and one thing led to another and...."

Dorothy's eyebrows practically disappeared into her hairline. "You mean he's a contractor. You just told me you weren't dating one. For heaven's sake, Mallory, what do you know about this man?"

She'd had essentially the same conversation with Duncan hours ago. If you could call it a conversation. But it might save the situation yet. "I know quite a lot about him, actually." To hide her face, she turned and poured water into the coffeemaker. "He's very good at what he does. He's good with his hands."

"I do not need to know the salacious details." Dorothy enunciated her *n*'s with scathing precision.

"I meant around the house, Mother."

"These are not exactly the qualities you should be looking for in a husband," she hissed, glancing down the hall.

"Who says I'm looking for a husband?"

"You should be. Women from Morrison stock do not let men live off them. They're too good for that."

Mallory choked back a defensive retort. Okay, so she was lying to her mother. That didn't mean Dorothy needed to talk to her this way. "Duncan's not living off me. He's self-employed."

"Yes, but what is he doing—moving in with you?"

Dorothy threw her hands in the air. "I just cannot believe you gave up a successful career and a wonderful man for a—a jack-of-all-trades who just walked in off the street. He could be a drug addict for all you know. A wife beater. A serial killer. Certainly he's a gold digger."

"Did he look like any of those things?" Mallory reached up for two mugs and poured coffee into them. She'd go without. She'd probably choke if she tried to drink anything.

"You can't tell by looking at a person."

"Exactly. And you can't tell he isn't a decent guy just by looking at him, either. Please don't question my choices, Mom. I'm twenty-eight and I'm pretty good at sizing people up after going through the SpendSafe thing."

Her mother stared at her, and Mallory realized what she'd done. She'd spoken up like an adult instead of taking it like a beaten child. No wonder Dorothy looked surprised.

"Questioning your choices? Is that what you think I'm doing?"

"It *is* what you're doing," Mallory said gently. "But what's best for me is up to me. You need to trust me. Trust that I'll take what you taught me and use it the right way."

She handed her mother the mug. Dorothy accepted it slowly. "I trust you." Her mother stopped. "Is that why you get so angry with me sometimes? And I don't hear from you for weeks?"

"It's hard to be in control and respected in the workplace, and then come home and have someone question your decisions and impose their wishes over yours. That was the biggest reason I broke up with Jon. I grew up a long time ago, Mom, but neither of you have really seen that—or seen me."

"Elaine says your buying this house was some kind of feminist reaction."

Mallory smiled. She made it sound like a skin rash. "She was partly right. I wanted to do something concrete on my own. I had the money, and I wanted this house. You know how sometimes you get that prickly feeling and an adrenaline rush, and you just know you have to do one particular thing? That's how it was for me."

"Is that how it was with—with—" Dorothy shrugged one shoulder in the direction of the stairs "—him?"

Duncan was a rush of an entirely different kind. "Kind of."

"I just want you to be safe. And not make the kinds of mistakes I did." Dorothy looked into her coffee as if she could read the future there. Or maybe it was the past. "It would really hurt to see you deserted, too."

"It's a little early for that," Mallory said. She paused. "You've done all right with us, you know, Mom. You did a good job." How had her mother's conversation transformed from her usual litany of Mallory's faults to this? She couldn't remember ever talking with her mother woman to woman instead of woman to child.

"Do you really think so?" Dorothy looked up. Her eyes glittered.

"Aw, Mom." Mallory reached out and hugged her. She smelled the familiar scent of Chanel No. 5 and thought of a frightened young woman with two small children and no income. The long years her mother had spent in night school. Most of all, she thought of her uncompromising insistence that both Elaine and Mallory get jobs to help pay their way through college. Her mother was a fighter. She'd done it for love. And she'd won.

Mallory could win, too. It was bred in her bones.

"Is that coffee for me?" Duncan's rough-edged tenor cut through her thoughts and she and Dorothy moved apart. The memory of last night elbowed reality aside. If not for her mother's presence and this unexpected bit of playacting, she was almost afraid to think what they might be talking about now. Or if they'd be talking at all.

His grin was full of sex and mischief, but it was for Dorothy's benefit, not hers. There was something in his eyes that told her they still had unfinished business. She dragged her gaze away from his mouth. It didn't matter whose benefit it was for. That smile was enough to scramble any woman's brains.

"So, Mrs. Baines, what brings you here this morning?"

Duncan leaned against the counter, his hip and arm bumping companionably against Mallory's. At least, she supposed it looked companionable. Every time he touched her, a *zing* traveled down that whole side of her body. He smelled like clean skin and worn denim, and his heat reached across the scant inch between them to mess up her thoughts even more.

Dorothy looked as though she were trying to read them like a hand of cards, to see if they were a winning combination. "I'm showing a house a couple of blocks over in twenty minutes, so I just dropped by to see if Mallory was free for dinner Tuesday night. But now it looks as though I'll need another chair." She directed a smile at him, the kind that Mallory suspected her clients got when they noticed there were stress fractures in the plaster from the earthquake tremors.

"For you, we're free," Duncan said. "Aren't we?" He gazed lovingly into her eyes, and for a moment Mallory forgot where she was.

"Sure," she said. What was the question?

"What time?"

"Seven. Drinks at six-thirty."

"We'll be there."

Dorothy gathered up her things and stood in the doorway, one hand on the screen door. "Has Mallory told you she has a sister?"

"We've met," Duncan replied, easy smile still in place. He slipped an arm around her shoulders, and she fought the urge to melt against his side. Or maybe she should melt. That was what she was supposed to do, wasn't it?

"Well, Elaine and Matt will be there. And one or two other people." Dorothy eyed them once more, and turned to go down the steps. "Bye-bye, then, until Tuesday."

They stood in the doorway like the all-American perfect couple until the sound of Dorothy's patent-leather pumps faded.

"I can hardly wait." Duncan's arm slid from Mallory's shoulder and he stepped away from her.

"What do you think you're doing?" Her shoulder felt cold. In fact, her whole body felt chilled. "Passing yourself off as my boyfriend—good grief, Duncan. Do you know what you're in for?"

The glance he shot her was businesslike in the extreme. "Looks like I'm in for a family dinner, and then maybe some peace and quiet. Doesn't anybody in your family ever call first?"

"Of course not. They're family. Do you call your mother before you visit her?"

"Yeah, I do."

"Oh. Well, if you want some peace and quiet, maybe you should go back out to your car." The cold seemed to be invading her tone, too. She didn't know why her mood had swung from languorous to dangerous. So she felt a little guilty about last night. He should, too. In fact, he should feel downright ashamed of the way he had moved in and insinuated himself into her life. "If my family wants to drop in, they can do it any time they like. They don't need your permission. They have mine."

"I can't sit in the car now. If your sister or your mom came back, it'd look weird."

"You could say we had a fight and you're sulking."

"I don't fight. And I never sulk."

And he didn't. Instead, he stalked back up the

stairs. The raised board at the entrance to her room creaked, and silence fell.

The kitchen suddenly felt close and hot. Mallory snatched her gardening gloves from beside the back door and stormed down the deck stairs. She grabbed the nearest cluster of prickly thistles and strangled it with both hands.

8

WOMEN, DUNCAN THOUGHT in disgust. You save their pretty little butts and what do you get? An invitation to move out. He'd done some pretty quick thinking, there, convincing that cougar Mallory called a parent that he was her boyfriend. He needed a cover story anyway, so his continued presence in the neighborhood wouldn't be remarked on if people got to talking over their back fences. Nobody would think twice if Mallory's boyfriend were trimming hedges or maybe even borrowing a tool, say, from Blake Purdue. At which point Duncan could get a look inside the guy's house.

Good plans, all of them. Until you got to that expression on Mallory's face—fear and amazement and horror all in one.

What did she have to be afraid of? Her mother? She should try sprinting across a parking lot twenty yards ahead of a client's crazed husband with a gun. *That* was something to be afraid of.

Was it him? Not after that kiss. In fact, if anybody should be turning pale, it was he, after being as much as told he was standing in for someone else.

Or not. He couldn't quite figure out what she was

thinking, which was par for the course. If he could, he wouldn't be in this situation.

A man has his self-respect, he thought sourly. He slouched in the bedroom chair that was becoming as familiar to his spine as the driver's seat of his car. His list of license plates now had names to match, courtesy of his information broker, including a confirmation that last night's visitor was indeed Hope LaCrosse. Instead of sitting here brooding, he should be organizing some serious surveillance on Purdue's associates. Talking to people. Getting out of here and putting a little distance between him and Mallory. In other words, working. Not mooning around her bedroom, sulking because she—

He stopped that train of thought. He never sulked. It was unprofessional and a sure way to lose his focus.

This boyfriend act was just that—an act. He wasn't looking for love. He'd been taken in by a pro in Denver, and he wasn't about to make the same mistake again.

You may not have the life you planned, a little voice in the back of his mind said, *but you have a pretty good one. And a woman like Mallory doesn't come along every day.*

Which was a good thing. He'd never get any work done if that were the case.

Great. Now he was answering himself. This place was making him crazy. Or maybe being so close to a woman who kissed like that was making him crazy.

Aha, said that annoying little voice, like a mosquito strafing his ear. *There's the reason for the boyfriend.*

You're so transparent. You're hoping she'll go from the act to the real thing.

Not a chance.

Duncan got up, suddenly too restless to sit and listen to himself anymore. That was the problem with an analytical mind. He couldn't fool himself even if he wanted to.

On the landing he stopped to listen. It was just as quiet inside as it was on the street. Maybe she was in her office. But there would still be some movement, the sound of the wheels on her chair, maybe, or the click of computer keys. She was probably outside in that cute little denim skirt.

No, wait a minute. She'd had on jeans and a sweatshirt when her mom had ambushed them. And if his eye was as experienced as he thought, there had been nothing under that sweatshirt.

Don't think about what she's wearing. It isn't good for you.

In fact, being here at all wasn't good for him. After that kiss, he was in mortal danger of losing his professionalism, his focus, his control. A smart guy would get out of here before he lost everything he valued about himself. He had enough names now to end the surveillance and move on to the next phase.

Time to wrap it up.

At the bottom of the stairs a stack of sandpaper lay ready for action. Most of the spindles in the railing had been sanded, but the last half dozen waited for someone to pay them some attention.

He paused, jingling the car keys in one hand. He

never sulked. He was a better man than that. The least he could do for a woman who had lent him home and hearth was to sand a few of her damn spindles. A parting gift. Then he'd go do some real work. Follow somebody. Yeah.

He grabbed a piece of the fine-gauge sandpaper off the top of the stack and began to rub it over the rough wood. At least this way he could get rid of some of this excess energy. Maybe he'd even wear himself out to the point where he could look at Mallory Baines without wanting to undress her.

And then he'd say goodbye.

MALLORY WORKED her way around to the side of the house, leaving little piles of weeds at intervals behind her. What she really needed to do was go inside and finish the trim. Or go shopping. Or talk to Carly.

She wondered if her friend's big blond protector had stayed the night. If so, maybe they'd like to come over for a little sanding party. No, she couldn't do that. Nobody was to know Duncan was here, even people who were supposed to be his friends. Well, too late for that. Her family knew, and it wouldn't be long before her friends did, as well. She should go in and behave normally, and he could take it or leave it.

She heard the front door close, and sat back on her heels. Well, well. Speaking of behaving normally, here came an apology. She waited for him to come around the corner, but instead, he climbed into his car and drove away without even a glance.

He'd taken her at her word.

Great. Now what was she going to say at dinner on Tuesday when she arrived dateless?

Her mother would say "I told you so" and Elaine would commiserate and offer hours of counseling over the phone while trying to weasel the facts out of her. Jon would undoubtedly hear about it, and before she was even dressed Wednesday morning, he'd be on her doorstep again, offering her a job and his oh-so-eligible self once more.

Darn Duncan anyway! What kind of guy would come up with a harebrained story like that and then abandon her to live with the epilogue?

That was probably his life. He probably invented any number of stories every day to mask what he was really up to—investigating people. It was a wonder he didn't get them all confused and have a major identity crisis.

She might know a lot of superficial things about him. Like the fact that he could kiss like nobody's business. Or that he looked sexy and dangerous with a day's growth of beard. Or that he knew the difference between chickweed and jasmine.

But she knew nothing about him under the surface except that he'd built model planes as a kid, and had a mother in Denver, whom he called before he came to visit. What kind of a relationship was that?

Not that she'd mind if her own mother would call before she came over, but things were sensitive enough on that front. If she insisted on a warning shot before a visit, their newfound understanding would probably disappear.

She slapped her gloves together to dislodge clinging soil, and laid them on the deck rail as she went into the house. She swung the door of her bedroom open, expecting to see it empty and virginal once more. The bed was neatly made. Her embroidered pillows, bought in a street market on a business trip to Bangkok, sat where they always did.

And his black, heavyweight duffel bag still sat on the floor next to the chair, with one shirt sleeve hanging out of the zippered opening. The camera was nowhere in sight.

Mallory sat on the bed and blew out a long breath that disturbed the unruly curls on her forehead. He would be back. That was good.

She didn't want to analyze her relief any further. Last night had been a mistake, a case of pheromones out of control. A relationship was a bad idea right now. She needed to find out who she was first, before she invested herself in someone else. If Duncan Moore treated her like a motel clerk, then she could treat him like a temporary tenant, nothing more. This pretend boyfriend thing was a bad strategy.

Or was it?

Granted, her mother probably thought she wasn't going to come up with a better candidate. But if Duncan acted the part of boyfriend, even a temporary one, Dorothy's social ambushes would stop. And Jon would quit coming around for sure, as soon as he got the word. So two good things could come of this.

The bad things were that she didn't know if she could go through with the act. The man was all come-hither sexiness on the outside and a closed door on the inside.

So what did she need an open door for? He was using her house and her bedroom window. He'd made it abundantly clear this morning that he'd seen last night as a mistake.

It had been. She'd just keep telling herself that until she believed it.

MMONDAY MORNING Duncan sat with his list of names and addresses in a parking lot that overlooked SiliconNext, where he'd followed Danny Barda. Barda had stopped at a convenience store on his way to work and covertly taken a small pink package from a guy leaning on an ancient hatchback.

Duncan made a note of the plate in his notebook. Interesting. So it looked as though Danny was receiving parts, too. Did that mean he was giving other people a percentage to bring him parts from their companies?

Following that train of thought to its conclusion, was Purdue the end of the line? Was there someone above him? Did the casino fit in somehow, or was Purdue simply shipping the parts to some overseas version of a computer chop shop?

He needed to get into the guy's house to see if he could find something to answer those questions. And then what he really needed to do was hand this case off to the cops.

The long slog through morning traffic, a short visit to his apartment and a longer one to his office, and the familiar rush and buzz of noise all around him had shaken him back to reality. No more of the fantasy life in Sleeping Beauty's castle. He'd broken promises to himself once too often, and like a fool, he still didn't know if he could trust Mallory Baines as well as kiss her. He couldn't have one without the other.

Scratch that. He couldn't have either one.

Time to bail.

He pulled his cell phone from his pocket and dialed SiliconNext. Barbara Mashita's assistant had her on the line in seconds.

"Duncan!" It sounded as if she'd run down the hall. "I was getting antsy, wondering when I'd hear from you."

"Got a minute?"

"Yes. Let me close my door." After a pause, during which he heard her say "Hold my calls, would you, Mel?" she came back on the line. "All right. What have you got?"

"I've got your suspect. But I have a feeling you're not the only one being ripped off. Just a feeling. No proof yet."

"You mean, there might be a ring or something?"

"Yeah."

"Nothing surprises me anymore. Who is it? From here, I mean."

"Guy named Danny Barda."

"Oh, no." Barbara's voice was soft with distress. "His sister works here, too. I took him on because they were practically destitute. They're both great assemblers."

"He's not destitute anymore. His buyer must be making it worth his while to take the risk."

"His buyer? You know that, as well?"

"A guy named Blake Purdue. Lives in Santa Rita. I've been watching him receive pieces at the end of every shift for a couple of days now."

"Can you prove it?"

"I've got pictures, but no proof of what's in the packages. But they're small and wrapped in pink plastic, like the one you showed me."

"And he might have people bringing him stuff from other companies. This makes me really angry, Duncan."

"I don't doubt it. Danny and his sister didn't come into the picture until Friday night, or I'd have called you sooner."

Friday night, before Duncan had kissed Mallory Baines and lost himself in her sweet, soft mouth and forgotten all about the investigation. He was definitely in trouble, here. He was going to wrap this up before he did something even more stupid than sanding her damn spindles just to see her smile again. "Sorry, what was that?"

"I said, I bet they're taking them from all over the Valley, so no one makes any one company too suspicious."

He marshaled his thoughts into order. "Except you."

"So now what do I do? Terminate him?"

"What is this, the Death Star?"

"Terminate. Fire. Relieve of his responsibilities. As you know perfectly well."

"No, don't do that," Duncan said. "Say you fire him and tell him you're going to file criminal charges. What does he do? He disappears before you pick up the phone to call the cops and you never see him again. We don't want him to reappear and do this to someone else."

"You're right. Of course you're right. What, then?"

"How far do you want me to go with this? You hired me to find your thief. I found him. You call in the cops, case closed." Just saying the words filled him with relief. He could pack up his duffel and escape before he got any deeper into—

"That might take care of the little guys, but this Purdue creep is still out there, raking in the profits. He's a threat to everything we've built here. I'm not going to let him get away with it, and that means neither are you."

Uh-oh. "You want me to stick with the case?" he said slowly. "See if I can come up with something to put him away?"

"Yes. I want him out of business. Then maybe he'll know how it feels."

"Hell hath no fury. Where's my old friend Barbara, the philanthropist? The caring CEO?" He was babbling, racking his brain to find a reason to refuse.

"Don't believe everything you read in the trade magazines. I care. Can't you tell I care?"

"I can tell, all right. Jeez. Don't you have a meeting to go to?"

"Melanie's giving me the look. Get back to work. And keep me posted."

"I always do." He turned the phone off and slid it back in his jacket pocket.

Great. Just when he thought he'd made it out of the frying pan, Barbara was going to pay him to jump back into the fire.

9

MALLORY CAME DOWN the stairs slowly, one hand on the banister. Fine sawdust backed up under her palm. Sawdust? She stopped. There had been six unfinished spindles. She knew that. She'd been doing a couple a week for an endless number of weeks. And now there were none.

Only one person could have done it.

For a moment, she was grateful. Then her old fears of domination and loss rushed in. Did he think she wasn't capable of this on her own? That she couldn't manage something as small as a spindle without his help? Logically she recognized that all men weren't like Jon. But this struck at the part of her that stood on that blurry border between renovating a house and making over a person.

Duncan had made her home, her room, and even significant portions of her body his own. She'd told him before, this place was her paint-by-numbers and she was the one who decided when things got done. Not him. Not anybody.

She'd talked herself into a fine temper by early evening when his car pulled up out front, tucking in between the plumbago bushes as if it belonged there.

When Duncan bounded up the staircase, she followed him into her bedroom.

He was writing in his notebook when she got to the threshold, and he looked up with a distracted expression. "Oh, hey. Everything all right?"

"No."

He made some more notes. "No?"

"You've crossed the line this time. You can close your book and take your stuff out of here."

Slowly he put the pen away. "What?"

"You heard me. We're done."

"What did I do?"

She crossed the room until she was nearly nose to nose with him. "I did my part. I helped you, I let you into my house, I gave you my room when you asked me to. I let you lie to my mother. I even let you kiss me. And what do you do?"

"That's what I'd like to know." He stood, eyes wide and innocent, his hands open, palms up.

Mallory refused to be taken in by the appealing picture he made. She was standing up for her principles here. "Don't patronize me! Did you think the little woman couldn't do it on her own? Did you think she needed the big, know-it-all man to get it finished?"

Silence filled the room. Duncan bent a little to look into her eyes. "Is this—is this about that bit of sanding I did this morning?" he asked at last.

"Yes!" She wanted to pound on his chest, feel him struggle, push him out of his calm, infuriating male reason and make him respond. "And I told you to stop patronizing me."

"I'm not patronizing you. All I did was finish off the job because it looked as though it needed doing. As a thank-you. Before I say—"

"You expect me to believe that?"

"You can believe it or not." He shrugged. "It's the truth."

She hated calm in a man. "Right, as if anything you've told me since you got here has been the truth. You know what? You're completely made up. Every person you meet gets a different guy. You think I need a handyman? You play handyman. You think I need a boyfriend? You play that, too. If I needed a scuba diver, there you'd be, in fins and a mask. What I'd like to know is, who is the real Duncan? When is he going to show up?"

He leveled a long, narrow look at her, a dangerous spark leaping behind his eyes. Good. She was getting to him in exactly the way he got to her. Finally some emotion was getting past the hall of mirrors he presented to the world.

"You want the real guy?" he ground out. "Not happy with the one standing here? Okay, how's this for real?"

He snaked one arm out, grabbed her around the waist and yanked her against him. Before she could drag in another breath, he crushed his mouth down on hers. She struggled in his grip, but he only pulled her closer while his tongue slid between her lips and invaded her mouth. Desire leaped out of the ashes of her anger and her knees went weak with the force of it. Soon his kiss became less punishing and more seductive. Both of his hands slid from her waist down over her lumbar curve and pressed her hips into his, holding her against a hardness that hadn't been there a moment ago.

Her hands, which had been fisted against his chest, uncurled and slid around his neck, one finding its way beneath the collar of his cotton shirt, the other into the hair at the nape of his neck. She wriggled closer and pressed the weight of her aching breasts into his chest. He groaned and took her mouth with renewed force.

She reveled in the feel of his arms around her, his fingers traveling her back with an urgency that echoed her own need to get even closer. This was real. This was Duncan, drinking her in as though he would never get enough, who wanted her, Mallory Baines, not as an accessory or a prize or even a motel clerk, but as a woman. The stark honesty of his passion told her so.

He lifted his head and they both gasped for air.

"Don't stop," she murmured, nuzzling the skin beneath his ear. She felt drunk with the scent and the heat of him.

He tilted his head back and planted both hands on her waist, as though he were going to push her away. She pressed closer.

"Mallory." The hands on her waist gentled. "I'm sorry. I shouldn't have done that."

"There are too many *shoulds* in my life. Don't add more." She nipped his ear, and he drew a quick breath.

"No. I have to wrap this up. I can't get involved."

She felt him swallow with difficulty as she tasted the skin at his collarbone, her mouth lingering with each slow kiss.

"You're sleeping here," she reminded him, touching his earlobe with the tip of her tongue. "You told my mother you're my boyfriend. You've kissed me three times, and you liked it. How much more involved do you want to get?" She ran her tongue along the rim of his ear.

He shivered. "Don't do that."

This time it was she who captured his mouth. For a moment she was afraid he wouldn't respond, that he would push her away, but his lips softened as his resistance crumbled, and she pressed her advantage. She had never attempted to seduce anyone before. Her success gave her a thrill of feminine power that made his response, as he gathered her back into his arms, even more rewarding.

This time when they broke apart, he made no move to push her away. Instead, he looked deep into her eyes. "Just to set the record straight, my sanding those spindles was not a declaration of war between the sexes."

She didn't want to talk about the spindles. In fact, she didn't even care about them. His kisses left her so hot all she could think about was how to get him out of his shirt so she could run her palms along his skin.

"Mallory?"

"Okay," she sighed. "Take your shirt off."

"A minute ago you wanted to throw me out of the

house." A smile crinkled the corners of his eyes. "I want to make sure you've forgiven me."

"If I forgive you, will you take your shirt off?"

"Will you promise not to threaten me every time I lend you a hand?" His hands slid from her waist. "I meant it when I said I was only trying to help. To say thank-you. Not to invade or push a power play on you."

His eyes were as honest as his lips had been a moment ago. This, too, was the real Duncan Moore. The man who made her toes curl and her body ache. Who made her skin hungry for his.

Lord, what was happening to her?

"I believe you," she said. "Kiss me again."

She reached up to touch his face, but he stopped her hand. His fingers wrapped around hers in a grip as serious as the expression in his eyes.

"What is it?"

"I need to ask you something."

"No, I'm not on the Pill," she quipped.

He huffed a laugh, and his grip on her fingers tightened spasmodically. "Go easy on me, Mallory. I'm trying to do the right thing, here."

"Those pesky ethics. Can't you put them on hold just for a minute?"

This time when he looked into her eyes, the seriousness had been replaced with longing. "I could, but that wouldn't be fair to you."

"Let me decide what's fair to me," she whispered. She put his hand firmly on her waist, slid her arms around his neck and touched his mouth with her own. "Like this."

She felt the tension in the back of his neck as he tried to resist, but then his arms went around her and she sensed the moment when he gave himself up to the pleasure they created together. The fire, banked for a moment while they had talked, flared up again. She sank into it and let it take her wherever he was prepared to go.

He pulled his mouth from hers, breathing as though he'd forgotten how. "Mallory. Stop. I can't think."

"What would you do a silly thing like that for?" He was as bad as a teenage girl. Stop. Go. Don't. Do.

"Because there's something I need to know."

Okay. Whatever it was, it must be a biggie. Nothing else would give a man superhuman control like this, unless he just wasn't as hungry for her as she was for him.

No, that wasn't right. His body had told her the truth on that score. She gave up and moved over to sit on the bed, putting a nice, cool six feet or so between them. "Okay. What is it?"

He remained by the window. "I need to know how close you are to Blake Purdue."

She stared at him. Blake Purdue? What on earth did he have to do with anything?

"How close I am?" she repeated. "A couple of hundred feet. He helps me out once in a while, like when I needed to paint the dining room. But as far as anything more, definitely not."

"He seems pretty interested. And you did go out last night."

She flushed. Now was probably not the time to explain the theory of reserve guys and the helpful function they served in a woman's life.

"He is interested. He's been interested ever since he moved in and found out I lived here. The very first time I met him, he was bird-watching in my backyard, under a bush. It scared the daylights out of me. I thought he was weird. But now I know better. The guy is like margarine on white bread—okay to have around, but not very interesting day in and day out."

Not like some people she could name, whose secrets begged to be found out and mulled over, where mutual discoveries added spice and zest to life. If his kisses sent her body into spice overload, what would making love with him do? She shivered with anticipation at the possibility.

He was still looking at her as if he weren't a hundred percent convinced.

"When he's around, does he share things with you? For example, things that happen at work, things he does with his friends, stuff like that?"

When were they going to stop talking and get back to kissing? She felt like telling him, *Duncan, you don't have to worry about the guy, honest,* but she didn't. Instead, she answered, "Not really, no. I don't even know where he works, except that it must be in manufacturing somewhere, because he comes home in electrostatic gear. But his friends are around all the time."

"What do you mean?"

She lifted her chin in the direction of the window where he stood. "People are always dropping in on him, even in the middle of the night. He must have the patience of a saint."

"Like your friend Hope."

Mallory frowned. "Hope is not having an affair with him. She must have been there delivering a message from her brother."

"That's what phones are for. Besides, he'd just seen her brother."

"Maybe he forgot something. I don't know. But she's not sleeping with him."

He glanced over his shoulder at the street, and his focus suddenly intensified. If she thought they were going to get off the subject of Blake and his friends, and back on to something much more interesting, she was disappointed. He grabbed the notebook off the chair and scribbled something in it.

"What is it?" Mallory joined him at the window. The same middle-aged man she'd seen on Thursday knocked on Blake's door. In his left hand he held a small pink package.

How weird. The pink stuff looked exactly like the electrostatic bags that computer parts came in. She'd seen hundreds of them during her career in the industry. What was this guy doing with—

The door opened, he slipped inside and, in less than five minutes, came back out and drove away.

The notebook in Duncan's hand didn't tell her much. Just the same list of license plates, only longer.

"I think you should give up on cheating spouses and think about computer parts," she said. "I don't like the look of that."

"What do you mean?"

She glanced at him, but he was gazing out the window at Blake's house. "Did you see that pink packet?"

"Yes. Do you know what it was?"

She shrugged. "I suppose it could be vegetables from his garden, but I doubt it. That stuff is thick, made especially to reduce static around memory sticks, so the circuits don't short out. And the only place you could get them would be a manufacturing operation."

He was silent a moment. "Any idea why that guy and your friend Hope would be bringing packages of parts to Blake?"

Hope, Mallory thought with a pang. She'd brought an identical package, pulled it out of the pocket of her lab coat. "Hope works swing, always has, so she can look after her mom during the daytime. She would have been getting off shift, if you add half an hour to drive over here." Cold apprehension and disbelief shivered over her skin. "This is bad. Something is seriously wrong if Hope—no, I can't believe it."

"Look, I really shouldn't be telling you this, but it's probably time I told you the truth. My client hired me to find out how the parts were getting out of the facility, and where they were going. Looks like we have the answers right here."

"That scumball," she whispered, glaring at Blake's house. "Why aren't you calling the cops?"

He fanned the pages of his notebook. "A little thing called proof. I need more of it than this. And my client doesn't want the cops involved in case Wall Street hears about it."

"Oh." Mallory felt a little deflated. "Yes, that would be a problem, all right. So what are we going to do?"

He put the notebook down and took both her hands in his. "*You* are not going to do anything. I'm the guy getting paid for this."

"But at least you trust me now, don't you?" She wanted him to trust her. She wanted to feel like part of his life. At the very least, she wanted to feel his arms around her again, holding her close, without the barriers of his work between them.

He was silent a second too long. "I'd like to feel that I could. Actually, I don't have much of a choice now. You figured it out and you could—in theory—walk across the street and tell Blake who I really am."

"Do you think I would do such a thing?" A needle of pain slid into her heart. Had he been working in the underworld so long he figured everyone was on the dark side, even a woman he had kissed with such passion?

"I'd like to think you wouldn't," he said.

Which, of course, was no answer at all.

10

DUNCAN LAY UNDER the borrowed blankets on the couch and listened to the faraway sound of gulls calling over the water. Mallory would never know how much willpower it had taken to step away from her soft invitation yesterday and not spill his whole heart to her. He'd wanted to do it. He'd started to let down a barrier, but then had thrown up a wall, like a reflex he couldn't control.

Bad enough that he was so transparent and so rattled by kissing her that she'd figured everything out with the inevitability of dominoes falling. He could only hope Purdue wasn't as smart.

Duncan had been a failure as a cop. He might be a pretty good P.I. But could he stand a chance as a lover?

There was a good reason he'd avoided relationships after the Denver debacle. He'd been deeply in love then, and it had blown up in his face. Even when he'd found out Amy was bucking for a partnership in the law firm that they'd identified as a nest of cocaine importers, he hadn't dropped her like a hot potato. His Amy would never be involved in criminal activity. Oh, no. Not the woman he was going to ask to be his wife.

He'd put his best into that relationship, and in the end Amy had laughed. At his dreams and hopes. At his stupidity.

At him.

Yes, the joke had been on him when she'd used the brains that had taken her to the top, skimmed the contents of his laptop, and run straight to the lawyers involved with every detail of his investigation. The case had crashed and burned, and Amy and her accomplices were now drinking piña coladas somewhere in the Caymans. Duncan had handed her the life she'd always wanted. And it had the benefit of not including him.

He shook the maddening memories away. The only thing that was real here was the job. He had to get himself back under control. That was vital, or he'd become as addicted to Mallory's smile and her lightning-quick mind and that delighted sparkle in her eyes as any street junkie. He'd lost it too many times now. If he wasn't careful, he'd find himself actually needing her kisses and the touch of her skin.

The problem was, he was still stuck with this boyfriend plan. He had to play it close enough to the edge to be convincing, yet far enough away that he didn't lose his footing. There would be no more playing boyfriend in private, though. He'd just have to get used to this unsatisfied hunger. It made him even more determined to get the job done and get out.

He flung the blanket off and pulled on his jeans and a T-shirt. While he started a pot of coffee, he attempted to banish stray thoughts of waking a warm, tousled Mallory with a kiss and a steaming cup, of her holding her arms out to him, of joining her in a tumble of sheets and discovering each of her curves in delicious succession with his lips....

Focus, dammit.

He walked outside into the cool, bright morning while he waited for the pot to fill. The sun had lifted above the pewter-colored rim of the ocean enough to reveal the home's shabby potential.

He took several deep breaths and channeled his thoughts into how a man could make himself useful around the place while he waited for Blake Purdue to slip up. One mistake was all he needed. Then he'd hand the case over to local law enforcement and be out of here.

The wraparound porch, especially in front, was the perfect project. The decking was spongy, the rail a threat to anyone who leaned on it. The gingerbread trim was broken, like torn lace on an old lady's dress. That would definitely have to be taken care of before Mallory painted. And if he happened to need some tools, he could walk over to Purdue's and see if he had some.

Brilliant. His mind was back on track, evaluating strategies. Normal.

When he went back into the kitchen for the coffee, she was drinking hers, both hands wrapped around the cup and her eyes closed in what looked like—he took another step—bliss.

She heard the screen door close and looked up.

"Obviously I should have assigned coffee to you days ago. What do you do with it that I don't?"

He shrugged. It was dumb to get too happy about producing that kind of look on a woman's face without even touching her. "I make it strong."

"So do I. But it never tastes like this. If you're going to stick around here, you have to do this every morning."

He could think of a few other things he'd like to do every morning. "Deal. I've been outside, checking around."

"For what?"

"Things I could do." He got the other mug and poured himself a shot. "Boyfriend things."

She leveled him a look. "Outside? I thought you wanted to be incognito. Not let anybody know you were here."

"I had to change my cover story when your mother arrived." His tone was wry.

"So normal boyfriend behavior is to work around the house. I get it. What did you come up with?"

"Quite a number of things. You've got your hands full."

"I've also got the time and the money."

"And the commitment." That was one more thing he liked about her, unfortunately. Sticking to a case was one thing. But renewing a commitment to something day in and day out, despite the obstacles, was another. "I noticed that your front porch could use some work."

She made a face. "I hope you didn't fall through. It makes a good trap for door-to-door salesmen."

"If you want, I could take a look underneath, do some repairs. And replace the gingerbread."

"First I need it to be safe. We'll work on pretty later."

"Practical. I like that in a woman."

She blushed, and looked so completely feminine and touchable he had the wild impulse to pull her into his arms for a proper good-morning kiss. Instead, he drained his mug and changed the subject. "How are you set for tools?"

"I have painting and finishing stuff spread all over."

"I meant a hammer and maybe a drill or a power saw."

"Oh, big boys' tools. You can check outside in the garage. Everything came with the house."

He nodded and beat a retreat out the door before he actually gave in to his impulses, and took an inventory of the contents of the garage. Besides her car, the garage held a number of boxes, all neatly labeled and stacked on portable shelving. In the back was a workbench, with hand tools circa 1940 piled haphazardly on a surface dark with age. He smiled.

He strolled down the block with his hands in his pockets, the picture of suburban ease. Blake Purdue's picket fence had a gate in the middle, but he stepped over it onto the front walk. He knocked on the front door and waited.

The door opened and Purdue peered out, T-shirt wrinkled and sweatpants sagging. "Hi."

Duncan flashed his best neighborly grin. "Morning. Hope I didn't wake you."

Purdue ran a hand through his hair. "Not really. What are you up to?"

Looking for stolen parts. "Getting an early start." He waved in the direction of Mallory's house. "Do you have a cordless drill? I'll bring it back as soon as I'm done."

Purdue looked puzzled. Maybe it was because he'd never heard of a cordless drill. "I thought contractors had all their own equipment."

"Yeah, well." Time for the cover story. "I'm not technically a contractor. We were just being discreet. If you've ever met her mom, you'd know why. I figured it was time I got to know her friends better." He gave him a winning smile and held out a hand. Purdue took it and gave it a quick, noncommittal shake.

"Discreet? What do you mean?"

The last thing Duncan wanted was to tick him off, make him think he was the loser in the game. "We're seeing each other. We don't want to make a big thing about it, though."

"If that's your car parked in front of her place, I'd say you were doing more than seeing each other." Purdue tried to turn it into a joke, but Duncan could tell the guy was burned. Not to mention observant. But to build an operation like his, Blake would have to be both observant and smart. Only a foolish detective would underestimate him.

And Duncan was no fool. Not anymore.

"So anyway, about that drill...?"

"I don't have one."

"That's okay. I can rent it. But I thought I'd ask." He stood there for another moment. Some guys would ask a man in for something to drink. Evidently Blake wasn't one of those guys.

"So are you really working around the place, or is it just a story for her mom?" Purdue asked.

"You've met her?"

"Once. That was enough. Her sister's nice."

"Yeah, I am working there. Have to earn my keep."

Purdue nodded without breaking eye contact. "There are names for guys who live off rich women," he agreed. "Wouldn't want that. How long are you going to be around?"

What was that supposed to mean? "We're going to give it a try, see how it works out. You know. No time limits."

"Tell her I'm still available to help if she needs me." Behind the words Duncan heard, *When she sees the light and dumps you.*

"I'll do that," he said. If he didn't like him before, he really, really didn't like him now.

"See you around." Purdue shut the door in his face.

Okay. Fine. No drill. No drink. No look in the house. He could live with that. There was still time to come up with Plan B. Next time he'd ask for something easy, like a hammer.

By late that afternoon he'd taken some measurements, arranged for a lumber delivery and talked the home store out of a couple of gingerbread samples for Mallory to look at. She was getting better results out of her boyfriend than Barbara Mashita was getting out of her detective.

He'd try the hammer tactic tomorrow, and if that didn't work, he'd have to seriously consider breaking and entering. Somehow, he had to find proof that Purdue actually had parts in his house. It would be nice to find out what he did with them, but that was beyond Duncan's scope.

Mallory stuck her head out the front door while he was on his hands and knees inspecting the supports under the porch. "Duncan?"

"Right here."

She looked over the rail at him. "Mom's expecting us in about an hour."

Mom? It was Tuesday. He'd forgotten about the family dinner. "Is this a formal affair?"

"I hope not. I'm just wearing this."

He straightened to have a look. She had on a cotton sheath dress in some kind of Hawaiian print. Fabric printed with hibiscus flowers emphasized her curves even more than usual. Her legs were bare, her hair twisted up in a way that made it puff around her face. A tiny breeze sent him a hint of her perfume, and he practically salivated.

"You look great." He sounded dazed, even to himself.

She was still for a moment, as if evaluating whether he meant it or not, then smiled. "We should leave about quarter after six."

"I'll be ready."

No way was he going to get through an entire evening playing boyfriend to a woman who looked like that. Maybe he could fake an injury. He looked for a rotten board he might conveniently put a foot through, then thought better of it. Injured investigators didn't get paid.

He'd gotten himself into this. Now he was going to have to go through with it.

Not for the first time, Mallory wished her mother lived in the Valley, so it would take a long time to drive through the hills to get there. A good hour, at least, in which to talk herself into this whole girlfriend act. Not that she didn't know how to be somebody's girlfriend, mind you. But where had the line between pretend and real gone yesterday, when she'd kissed Duncan Moore and felt the honesty of his response? How was she supposed to act after something like that?

Her mother's smile faltered as she opened the door, but as a Realtor, no doubt she was used to making the best of a bad thing. "Hi darling. You're right on time, as usual. Ah, Douglas...?"

"Duncan," he said with a grin that would charm a dollar right out of a skinflint's wallet.

"Yes. Duncan. Douglas was one of your boyfriends from college, wasn't he, Mallory?"

Mallory was saved from a reply by a tackle around the legs. "Auntie Mal!" her nephew squealed.

"Hi, Kevin." She hugged the six-year-old close. "What's happening?"

"*Alien Destroyers.* Nana bought it for me." Kevin wiggled away and went to load the game into the computer.

"Well, well. From switchplates to dates. Working on more than the house, I see." Elaine, in white capris and a billowy linen shirt, practically bounded across the room to shake Duncan's hand. "How are you?"

Mallory rolled her eyes. Her sister might as well come right out and say, "Nice hunk, Mal. Is he good in the sack?"

"Elaine," she began, in hopes of forestalling a disaster, "don't say anything about—"

"I can't tell you how happy I am you're here," Elaine gushed. "Anyone who makes my sister lie has got to be someone special."

Why did she have to be born into such a family? Mallory hid her burning face in hugs from her brother-in-law, Matt, and her niece, who was reading on the couch.

"Hey, Holly. Is that a good book?"

"It's *The Babysitters Club.* I've read this one." Holly looked up at Duncan, who was talking to Matt. Something he said made her father laugh, and Holly glanced at Mallory. "Is that your boyfriend?"

"Yes." She admitted it reluctantly. She could lie to her mother with hardly a qualm, but lying to her niece was another matter.

"You don't sound very sure about it."

"Well, he is."

Holly went back to her book while Mallory tried to squelch her guilty feelings. So many people saying they were one thing, yet doing the opposite. Duncan. Blake. Hope LaCrosse. Herself. Could anyone be trusted anymore? And if she felt this way, what must Duncan be thinking?

The doorbell rang again, interrupting her thoughts, and Mallory glanced at her mother. Wasn't this supposed to be a family party? The guilty glance Dorothy shot her as she hurried to answer it should have warned her. When she heard Jon's voice in the hall it all came clear.

She grabbed Elaine's elbow. "What is he doing here?"

"Ow, let go. How should I know?"

"Mom knew I was bringing Duncan. What was she thinking?"

"She can invite whomever she wants to her own house, Mal. Don't overreact."

"Who's overreacting?"

Jon came in with Dorothy on his heels. His hair was the latest cutting-edge style, with the front designed to curl rakishly over one brow. Instead of the khakis and golf shirt that were his leisure uniform, he wore crisp jeans and a white collarless shirt. He looked like a well-fed artist.

"What's with the new look?" Elaine whispered.

"Who knows? Maybe he's dating an undergrad and the golf shirts weren't a hit."

Jon made the rounds of the room as if he belonged there, while Mallory sensed Duncan's presence behind her, solid and warm. As Jon reached them, Duncan slid an arm around her waist, pulling her gently against his side.

"Mallory."

"Hello, Jon. What a surprise."

"I hope you don't plan on leaving before dinner. Your mom invited me several days ago. Last week, in fact."

Before she'd dropped over to invite them. Had she been planning to set her up again, and when Duncan appeared on the scene, decided it would be less embarrassing to go through with it than to back out? Did she want to line the two men up, so Mallory could comparison-shop and make the obvious choice?

Duncan stuck out his right hand, his left still firmly around Mallory's waist. "Duncan Moore. I don't believe we've met."

Jon took in the arm and the possessive stance, and Mallory deliberately relaxed against Duncan's side. It wasn't hard to do. In fact, it felt pretty good.

"Jon Easton. I run development for Ocean Tech here in Santa Rita. We do chips for some of the big computer companies in the Valley."

Duncan smiled. "No kidding. I do chips for Mallory. She says my nachos are the best on the planet."

Mallory had never seen Jon goggle before. It made him look almost human.

"Mallory? Have you been keeping secrets from us?" His voice was weak.

"Yes, she has," Dorothy put in. She handed Mallory a glass of white wine, and Jon a glass of red. "Duncan is the best-kept secret in this family since Christmas of 1977."

"Yeah?" Duncan put his empty hand in his back pocket. "What happened then?"

Mallory spoke quickly. She felt like the kid with his fingers in the dike, trying to stop the verbal leaks. "I'll tell you la—"

"That was the year my rat of a husband surprised us with his bimbo girlfriend and disappeared," Dorothy said crisply.

"No kidding. Did you off him or what?"

The silence widened like a crevasse at their feet. Finally Dorothy managed, "Did I what?"

"You said he disappeared." Duncan grinned. "I thought maybe you did him in and buried his body in the nearest sand dune."

Mallory wondered if it was too soon to leave.

"No, I did not," Dorothy said. "I had children to bring up. But I certainly thought about it."

"Mother!"

Dorothy shot Elaine an annoyed glance. "A woman's entitled to her own feelings. Those were mine at the time. Duncan, what would you like to drink?"

"Red, please."

Mallory forced her neck and shoulders to relax. She should have remembered her mother was a fighter. Obviously something elemental in Duncan struck a similar chord in her. Or maybe he was just very good at reading people in his line of work, and once again presented the facade he thought Dorothy wanted to see. She took a hefty swallow of her wine. Please God, let her get through this without anyone discovering they were both there to tell a lie.

11

THE SCORE WAS Duncan one, Jon one. Duncan balanced his plate of pasta and mussels on the redwood deck rail and resisted the primal urge to check the barbecue. Elaine's husband, Matt, clumsily assisted by Jon, probably wouldn't thank him for pointing out that the fish ought to have been cooked on a sheet of foil. Then they wouldn't be scraping it off the grill with a spatula and trying to save chunks big enough to serve. Duncan preferred mussels any day, and Dorothy certainly knew what she was doing with them. He nudged Mallory's elbow.

"Your mom puts on a great feed."

She nodded glumly. "The greatest show on earth, that's my family."

"Come on. They seem pretty normal to me." Not that he'd know much about it. He was so far from his mom and sisters, who were in Colorado, that he'd missed most of his nephews' childhood. His brothers-in-law hardly knew him. For the first time, Duncan wondered if his strategy for success in investigation wasn't doing more harm than good as far as his family were concerned.

As if she'd read his mind, Mallory asked, "How long has it been since you saw your mom?"

He thought for a moment. "Two years? Three?"

"That's a long time."

"If she needed me, she'd call." He hoped. Or had he made a point of encouraging her to call one of the girls first because they were closer? Had she ever really called and asked him for anything?

"Do you get on well with her?"

This was getting a little uncomfortable. "Yeah, I guess. We've had our differences, but so have you and your mom."

"True. But we seem to be able to talk through our problems lately. I wonder why?"

"Maybe because you're..." He trailed off. This was really getting personal. Maybe he should get some more wine.

"Because I'm what?"

Too late to back out. "Because you're more *you* now."

"More me? You mean, more of a person?" Her smile was a little sad.

"You weren't exactly chopped liver before. Maybe you've started to become the person you were meant to be, and she senses that."

She put her fork down and turned to him with a look he'd never seen before on any woman's face— penetrating yet completely vulnerable. "That is, without a doubt, the nicest thing anyone has ever said to me."

For a moment he squelched the overwhelming urge to take her in his arms. But he was her boyfriend. He could do that, right here in front of her mother and everybody. He put his fork down and threw caution to the wind, and she nestled against him as though she belonged there. For five sweet seconds he felt as if he had a place in this world, as if the two of them created a little island of safety and togetherness. A place he could almost get used to.

Out of the corner of his eye, he saw Jon's head go up, and the piece of fish he was trying to maneuver onto the spatula tilted and fell through the grill onto the coals. Self-preservation whispered that it might be smart to loosen up on the grip and step away from Mallory. Instead, he ran the flat of his hand slowly down her back and smiled.

"Care for some salmon?" Jon held a plate of fish fragments in one hand and a spatula in the other.

"Not for me," he said.

"Mallory? I cooked it the way you like it."

She liked it like this?

She pulled away and turned back to her plate. "No, thanks, Jon. I've got plenty here." She poked at a mussel with her fork, and twirled a strip of linguini around it.

"Come on. It was fresh off the wharf this morning. And you probably haven't had any since we made it at our place that time."

"You're right. I haven't." From her tone, *that time* may have had something to do with it.

Jon put the plate on the table and joined them at the rail. "This is a nice place, isn't it? The West Coast redwood style is a bit dated, but it's still worth a bundle."

"Mom's happy here." Her voice seemed a little subdued as she wound every last bit of the linguine in a perfect coil around the mussel.

"Is this where you grew up?" Duncan asked.

Mallory shook her head, but Jon answered. "No, the girls grew up over on the east side. Little postwar place. I hear they're going for three hundred K these days, as fixer-uppers."

"I was asking Mallory." He kept his smile firmly in place, his tone gentle.

"You can ask me. I think I know as much about her as anyone," Jon said.

"No doubt. But I asked her."

"Do you have some kind of problem?"

Mallory stiffened. "Jon."

"I don't know where you met this guy, Mallory, but if you want my opinion, he could use a little help with his social skills."

"Ah. I do admire yours." Duncan's tone was silky.

"Damn right. And any time she wants, she knows I'm here for her."

"You know, it's rude to talk about someone behind her back." Mallory turned around to face them, her plate gripped in both hands.

"I'm just making it clear that I'm supporting you," Jon said.

Duncan had to hand it to the guy—he really believed what he was saying. Jon's eyes were soft as he looked at Mallory.

"You are not," she said. "If you're going to squabble, take it somewhere else, not at my mother's house." And she walked through the open sliding door into the dining room.

He thought Jon would follow, but instead, her ex leaned one arm on the rail, mirroring Duncan's pose. "She tends to misunderstand." Jon watched her for a moment, then turned back to him. "What exactly is it you're doing here?" he asked.

Duncan shrugged. "I'm her date."

"Is that all?"

"Are you playing surrogate father, or what?" Duncan smiled, so Jon could take it as a joke if he wanted, and give them both an out. "Want to know if my intentions are honorable?"

Jon narrowed his gaze. "I'm not in the mood to play word games."

Obviously the guy had no sense of humor. Mallory was well rid of him. "I'm not in the mood for threats. I'm her date. Get over it."

"I'm a presence in her life, Moore. I asked her to marry me. Get that clear."

"Fine, but as I understand it, that deal fell through. I'm a presence in her house, and at the moment, that's what matters, isn't it?"

Jon paled. "What?"

"We're living together, in case Dorothy hasn't told you. So if you're a presence in her life, I suggest you get used to me."

"Liv—? Living tog—?"

"I'm going to get some more of those mussels." He sauntered toward the dining room, half expecting a spatula to bury itself in his back.

"Mallory?" he called softly as he slid the glass door shut behind him, shutting out the conversation and the clink of silverware as everyone ate out on the deck. The dining and living rooms were empty. So was the kitchen, although her plate, neatly scraped, was in the sink. He walked down the hall. No one in the office and bathroom. Or the master bedroom. That left the guest room.

"Mallory?" The door stood partly open, and he pushed it the rest of the way. She stood by the window, looking out at a dwarf palm in the front garden. "Are you all right?"

"Why is it that men have to assert territorial rights? Is it nature or nurture?" Her back was to him, her tone conversational, but one arm was wrapped around her middle, and the other hung by her side, her hand fisted.

"Look, I'm sorry if I made you uncomfortable. The guy needed his ego clipped."

"That's not your job."

"Are you defending him? Two points for him."

"This isn't a basketball game." She turned to face him. "It's a family barbecue. There isn't supposed to be a winner or loser. This is pretend. Remember?"

The adrenaline rush when Jon had challenged him hadn't been pretend. The desire that sizzled through him at the sight of her wasn't pretend. Her perfume was fogging his brain with its tropical scent, making him forget what was real and what wasn't. Or maybe it was the sense of relief and possibility that had filled him since she'd told him there was nothing between her and Blake Purdue.

He breathed deeply, his face close to her hair. "You smell good."

"Don't change the subject."

"We're talking about pretend and real. And reality is that you smell good. See? I can tell the difference." He nuzzled the skin below her ear.

"Don't."

"Don't what?" She even tasted good. Such soft skin. Did she taste this good all over?

"Don't remember...." Her voice faded away on a breath as she turned, and suddenly her mouth was opening under his like a flower. She made a little noise in her throat that fired him even more. He pulled her tight against him and she wriggled to fit between his thighs.

"You feel good, too," he said, and took her mouth again. He caressed her tongue with his and felt the electric charge of desire as she responded, teasing with an advance, inviting with a retreat. The pressure of her hipbones against his excited him unbearably, and he couldn't help a primal rhythm as he pressed a hand against her spine.

He was drowning in her kiss, in the feel of her body under his hands. She lifted one knee as if she wanted to crawl up his body, and he slid his other hand down her thigh. Short dress. Soft skin.

His mind emptied of anything other than merging two beings into one. Of getting so close that her skin would become his flesh and he would be completed and satisfied at last.

He found her zipper and pulled it down. Her dress loosened and fell forward off her shoulders.

Black lace lingerie. Desire pooled in his groin, heavy and hot. Her head fell back as he buried his mouth in the hollow of her throat and began to taste his way south. The erotic black tracery lying on her skin blurred in his vision. Had she put it on hoping that he would see it? Or did sexy bits of lace and satin hide under her practical clothes all the time? Either way, the thought was wildly exciting.

Taut, creamy curves rose from the fragile restraint of the lacy cups. His tongue slid into her cleavage and he felt the heat rising off her skin. She gasped and her fingers tightened on his shoulders. So she liked this as much as he did. He tasted every inch of exposed curve, holding back, the anticipation building.

"Duncan," she whispered. "Oh, yes."

She did something with her shoulders and one of the black straps fell down her upper arm. With his chin, he nudged the stiff cup down, and her nipple popped into view. With a growl, he tasted it, felt the shock of the pleasure ripple through her body, and he sucked it into his mouth. His blood felt thick with heat and desire, pounding its way through his veins.

"Beautiful," he mumbled, and nibbled the sweet, rigid fruit, suckling, pulling, making her gasp.

Somehow he had backed up against the narrow little bed, and he bent his knees, pulling her onto his lap. He heard nothing but the soft, inarticulate sounds she made, felt nothing but the urgency of his erection and the flesh under his tongue, saw nothing but this woman whom he'd desired from the beginning. He explored the horizon of the second cup, and was rewarded as her areola came into view. She clutched the back of his neck as he swirled his tongue beneath the lace and captured her nipple, devouring it with days of pent-up hunger.

She shook his shoulders with both hands. "Duncan!"

"Like that, do you?" he mumbled. He'd do anything she wanted. All he needed in the whole world was her and somewhere where they could be horizontal, and he'd be happy to stay there forever. He'd—

"Duncan, someone's coming!"

Damn.

She adjusted the bra and he reached around her. The zipper gave a tiny metallic scream as it raced up its track three quarters of the way and jammed.

"Let me." She spun off him and reached behind for the zipper. "It's stuck!"

"Here." He pulled the clip from her hair and fluffed the chaos of curls over the vee of bare skin at her nape just as her mother pushed open the door.

12

MALLORY DROVE HOME on automatic, all the important parts of her brain and body focused on the man in the passenger seat.

Desire sluiced through her at the thought of what his lips and tongue had been able to do in those few minutes. She'd been so close to orgasm that it had been nothing short of a miracle that she'd heard her mother's voice in the hallway. When Dorothy had walked in moments later, she'd seen nothing more than the two of them standing by the window. She hadn't seen the undone zipper, the erection Duncan had tried to hide by keeping his back to the door, the heated flush of arousal staining Mallory's face.

The arousal hadn't gone away. It made her bra feel tight and her underpants damp.

By the time they got to the last traffic light, she felt ready to combust. Duncan's left leg looked relaxed, but every time she reached for the gearshift, her hand brushed his knee. He had one arm draped over the open window frame, but his other hand lay on his thigh, within reach of hers.

As the light changed, she suddenly realized what her fingers were doing to the knob of the gearshift. Duncan swallowed audibly, and straightened as she accelerated down the last block and pulled into her garage.

Frustrated desire swung in dizzy circuits from her brain to her heart to the places he had brought alive with such consuming intensity. There was no way she was going to allow him to start something like that and not finish it, no matter how subdued he'd been on the drive home.

She almost wondered if he was going to run for his car or take a long walk on the beach. Instead, he followed her up the stairs. The air between them crackled with the unspoken, making the skin on her back prickle.

She flipped on the lamp in her room and went to the old-fashioned armoire, stepping around his duffel as if it were part of the furniture. She could feel his gaze between her shoulder blades.

Was he never going to speak? Or was he going to pretend that those few minutes in her mother's guest room hadn't happened?

Mallory turned to face him. "So are we back to business as usual, or are we going to talk about this—this thing between us?"

He stared at her, as if he couldn't decide whether to kiss her or make a break for safety. "This thing. You mean, whether I think you're involved with Blake?"

She took her time wetting her lips, and was gratified to see his gaze lock on her mouth. "No, whether I think I'm involved with you."

"We haven't straightened out the ethics yet." It

sounded as if he had trouble pronouncing the words. His voice was almost slurred.

She toed off her sandals. "I see. You kissed me. You broke the rules. But what if I kiss *you?* How unethical is that?"

If it weren't for the hunger in his gaze that gave the lie to the stiffness of his shoulders, she'd never have the courage to go through with this. But his inability to look away from her face made her brave. She turned and presented her back to him.

"Unzip me?"

Silence resounded in the room like a shout. "No." His voice sounded strangled.

"All right." She reached behind her and ran the zipper down halfway—enough to reveal the clasp of her black bra—then reached around at a different angle to undo the rest.

He swore in a half whisper. Her back felt cold, exposed. *Come on, Duncan. Don't leave me hanging like this.*

For five seconds that felt like eternity, they stood frozen in place as he seemed to struggle with something inside. Then he moved. His hands slid around her from behind, embracing her and pushing her dress off her shoulders at the same time. It slipped down her body to her feet, and she stepped out of it.

He walked her backward until the bed stopped their progress, and he fell sideways, pulling her with him so they were both lying on their sides. The warm brocade comforter puffed up around them.

He propped himself up on one elbow and looked at her. "How unethical do you want this thing to get,

Mallory?'' His voice was rough, the light in his eyes kindled now to a burning heat.

That light, the intensity in his tone, made up for those five seconds in spades. In answer, she pulled his head down and kissed him.

The lamplight glinted off his hair, turning the tip of each strand gold. He slid an arm around her and pulled her to him, settling her against his hard chest.

If nothing else, this was real. The heat in her blood, the hardness of his body, the demand of his mouth—those were real. He might be able to give her nothing else. Well, it was worth the risk. She'd go with that and let the rest fall where it would.

"Real," she whispered, dipping her head to catch his mouth as he plucked kisses along her throat.

"Real what?"

"Real unethical," she amended.

He dipped his head and stopped her, his lips a breath from hers. "Funny girl. Real gorgeous. Mouth." He kissed her. "Skin." He nuzzled her neck and shoulder. "Breasts."

He touched his tongue to the first hint of her cleavage, and she sucked in a soft breath. Her nipples were rigid, her breasts aching so she felt as if she were going to burst out of her bra. He brushed a lace-covered nipple with his mouth, and she gasped.

"Sensitive," he whispered. "I like that." With infinite gentleness, he bit one, taking the hidden hardness between his teeth and nibbling it. She moaned, the huskiness of his voice giving her almost as much pleasure as his skillful mouth.

Her temperature rose as he licked the curves of her breasts above the lace. "I want to taste you without any interruptions this time," he whispered as his tongue slid into her cleavage. "Let me?"

Her yes was a thread of sound on the still, midnight air. She sat up, straddling him, and combed her fingers through his hair, stroking his neck and spreading them flat on his shoulders under his shirt. He reached around her and undid the clasp of her bra, and some elemental surge of feminine power made her arch her back as he gazed at her. The bra, forgotten, dropped from his hand.

He sat up and braced himself against the pillows. Almost reverently, he filled his hands with her breasts, palming their weight with a groan of pleasure. He bent and circled one areola with his tongue and her breathing quickened with anticipation. "Do you like this?" he asked, his lips against her skin.

"You make me feel so good," she whispered, eyes half-closed, lips parted. She looped her hands loosely around his neck.

He moistened the other breast with his tongue, blowing gently on her nipple but not touching it.

"Lovely," he murmured. At last, he allowed himself to taste her nipple, and she shuddered at his restraint. She was filled with the need to give him as much pleasure as he gave her, to spend all night exploring each other's bodies and learn the secrets he kept behind the facade.

He drew her nipple deep into his mouth and suckled, rolling his tongue around the sensitive nerve endings, and she groaned and tossed her hair back. She squirmed in his lap, gripping his hips with her thighs, riding his erection with uninhibited eagerness.

"Your nipples are like blackberries," he whispered, filling his mouth and suckling. "Juicy. Sweet."

"You really like them?" Her voice was breathless, high.

"Like them? Girl, you are a feast." He dropped kisses down the taut curves of her cleavage. "There isn't a man on this planet who wouldn't love them. You are beautiful. Just looking at you across a room makes me hard."

In answer, she drove herself onto his erection and, even through her panties and his jeans, she could feel how close he was to explosion. He hooked his fingers over the lacy waistband and pulled her panties off, and she attacked the buttons of his jeans. When their clothes lay on the floor, he pulled her back in his lap.

"Now. Where were we?"

"You were telling me I was beautiful. I don't think you were finished." She tilted his face up with both hands and traced his lower lip with her tongue.

"You're right." He kissed her deeply, then dropped random kisses on her shoulders and throat as he spoke. "That very first day you let me in here. Remember?"

"Yes," she sighed.

"You stood by the window with the sun behind you. Do you have any idea what that did to me?" He nuzzled her skin.

"Tell me."

He traced the silhouette of her breasts with his tongue, with a long, sensual stop at her nipples. "I could see these beautiful shapes, and the shadow of your nipples. So erotic." He sucked blissfully. "Do it more often."

She purred with pleasure and trapped his erection under her, stroking its length with creamy wetness.

"You'd like that," she whispered. "Walking around the house with nothing on."

"I like the mystery. Clothes. No bra." He stroked her thighs, his hands roaming slowly to the soft skin at the very apex of her open legs. "I need to be inside you. Now. Please?"

"Yes." Her voice was dreamy as she stroked him with her wet heat, sliding up and down his shaft with the sinuous movement of a cat.

"I need to get something," he said through his teeth. He scrabbled for his jeans, fished the condom out of his wallet, and ripped the wrapper off. She lifted herself up long enough for him to put it on, then settled on him again. "Not so fast." He slipped his hand between their bodies and found her clitoris, swollen with her desire. He touched her and she jumped. "So sensitive," he whispered. "So ready for me."

He stroked her with tiny featherlike strokes, and suckled her breast. "Everywhere at once," she moaned. He rose to meet her as she sheathed herself on him in one smooth motion.

He cried out and she gasped, surrounding him, inviting his rhythm as his hips involuntarily began to pump. She had never been so enveloped by pleasure, her nipple under his circling tongue, his body buried in hers, his finger sure on the center of her.

She cried his name as she convulsed around him. Her muscles fluttered in waves, and with a shuddering stroke he exploded.

He collapsed onto the pillows, his arms still wrapped around her. She snuggled against his side and he gathered her close.

If he even dared to move, she thought, dazed, she would tie him to the bedposts with her own scarves.

Thank heavens Jon was out of her life. Imagine going through the next sixty years never knowing how good it was supposed to be. Duncan was a giver, putting her first, enjoying her pleasure because it added to his own. She'd never experienced that before. She tilted her head and watched his eyes flutter closed, the sometimes harsh outlines of his face beginning to relax. His hand stroked her back slowly, hypnotically.

Where was all this going to lead? She reached over and snapped off the lamp. The dark fell like an overstuffed quilt, blotting out the real world and leaving her with her thoughts and the solid feel of his shoulder under her head. His heart beat under the gentle hand she laid on his chest, as if willing him to stay.

Give a man a bathroom and he takes a whole house. Give him a kiss and he takes your whole body. Give him your body and heaven only knows what he'll take.

THERE WAS SOMETHING about the way she slept that drew Duncan's attention from the street, where it be-

longed, to the bed. Maybe it was the childlike vulner-
ability of her upflung hand. Or the tumble of hair on
the pillow. Or maybe it was just that it was getting
harder by the minute to do his job instead of what he
wanted to do, which was go over there and kiss her
awake.

He was beginning to seriously dislike the view from
this damn window.

He glanced at his watch. Six forty-five. A car he
hadn't seen before rolled up to the curb a block from
Purdue's house, and a man he recognized as Danny
Barda got out. He stuffed something in the pocket of
his jacket. Duncan saw a flash of pink plastic, and his
finger tightened reflexively on the camera's shutter.
He couldn't be sure he'd got the shot, but at least it
was more than he'd captured during the other drops.

There was only one way to confirm what was in
those packages. If he couldn't get into Purdue's house,
he was going to have to stop one of the couriers on the
way there and shake something out of him.

Mallory stirred, and a tug deep inside demanded he
go over there and slide under the covers next to her.
Resolutely he focused the camera and got a good head
shot as Blake admitted Danny to the house. He wished
they'd do the transaction on the back porch for once,
so he could get a clear shot of it. Then he'd have his evidence and he could concentrate on his life.

And what wasn't in it.

With Purdue's door shut for a few moments, Duncan's gaze returned to the bed with the accuracy of a
compass needle.

Last night had been a revelation. Not just the sheer sensual pleasure of it, although he hadn't realized it could be that deep, that consuming. No, it was discovering depths to his own sensuality through her, where giving her pleasure increased his own in measures he hadn't known existed.

It was enough to make a man rethink his strategy. Ever since Denver, he'd been a lone wolf, working on his own, calling for help only when he'd run out of choices. Amy had taught him that if nothing else. Trust no one. Watch your back. Do it yourself.

That worked pretty well in business. But maybe it wasn't such a great philosophy for personal relationships. Maybe it was time to forget the lessons Amy had burned into his psyche and pay some attention to the ones the woman in the bed had to offer.

He could reconnect with his family, for starters. His mother would treat him as if it had been two weeks instead of two years since the last time he'd called for anything other than an emergency. Jen and Kari would punish him for all of ten seconds, then ask him when he was coming to Colorado.

But what about Mallory?

He thought he'd gone into this as honestly as he could, but he knew now it was just a mask he'd put on an unpalatable truth. She was right to call him the man of many faces. He needed every one of them. Okay, he'd admit it. He was the one who was afraid.

Afraid to trust. Afraid to give. Maybe the case was just an excuse. Maybe the habits he'd built up as a protective wall had turned into a prison. Last night had taken a chunk out of the wall. What about the rest of it?

He was pretty much convinced that Mallory wasn't involved with Purdue. Could he start with that, add amazing sex, and chip away at the wall? Was that so hard?

Not if you enjoy turning your life inside out and starting over. Again.

The bedroom door creaked and he tensed. It swung open enough to allow Kiko to swivel around it and jump up on the bed.

"Duncan?" Mallory murmured as the Siamese planted herself in the soft angle between her thigh and ribs, just where Duncan wanted to be right now.

Damned opportunist.

He glanced outside at a movement across the street. Barda returned to his car and drove away. When Blake left at seven on the dot, as usual, Duncan laid the camera on the floor.

Mallory had rolled onto her stomach. The duvet had slipped down, baring her shoulders. He moved softly to the bed, shucked off his jeans and slid under the covers.

Kiko shot him an evil look and swatted his hand. Duncan pinched her paw gently in a fold of fabric, and the cat leaped off the bed and retired to the window seat, where the first rays of the sun dappled the fabric.

"Are you working?" Mallory mumbled against his chest.

"I was. Not now. This is strictly pleasure."

HE KISSED HER fully awake, taking his time about it. She'd been dimly aware of him at the window, and of the cooling space beside her that should have had him in it instead of the cat. There was something to be said for psychic suggestion, she thought as she met his tongue with her own.

She'd projected *come to me* and he had, even when she'd figured he'd withdraw and go and do something practical. She was wet and ready for him. Just knowing he was in the room could do it, as she'd proved over and over the past several days. His mouth on her skin, the rasp of his unshaven jaw against the curve of her breast, the way her smooth calf slid against his rough one all added up to an erotic experience she could really get addicted to.

He suckled her nipple and she stiffened at the pleasure of it. To say he enjoyed her breasts was an understatement. It was obvious he gloried in them—and he made sure she knew it by making her blood heat and the desire race from his wonderful mouth to the softest, most secret place that waited so impatiently for him. For the first time she was glad she'd inherited Great-Grandma Baines's figure. If she could give Duncan half the pleasure he gave her, she was glad.

His lips lingered on her skin. "You taste like me," he murmured, kissing her navel.

"Duncan?"

"Mmm?"

"What are you doing?" Her voice quavered as he moved even lower, dragging the duvet and baring her to the cool air. She welcomed it. She was on fire. But—

"I'm seeing if you taste like me anywhere else." His

voice rasped, and then his tongue slid into her most secret place, the place he'd possessed with his body only hours ago.

She gasped and clutched his hair.

"Let go, darling," he murmured. "Let me taste you."

Gently he moved her trembling thighs apart, and she nearly flew to pieces as his tongue worked its magic. She forgot how vulnerable she felt, and was conscious only of his slow savoring of every fold and every secret. Unerringly, he found the last secret of all, and in seconds she exploded against his mouth. The sound of his name filled the room.

He gathered her up as she gasped for breath. "Need you inside me," she begged, and wrapped her legs around his hips.

"One second." His voice was muted with what she could only guess was a Herculean effort to hold back as he tore another condom open. Then he slid inside her, filling her, giving her what she wanted. Her satisfaction had been so complete that she needed nothing more than to take him to the same pinnacle and send him over the edge. She clenched her muscles and his eyes popped open.

"Mal—do that again—"

As he moved in and out she stroked him from the inside. His gaze locked on hers and her eyes told him he wasn't alone in that high, breathless place. She was right there with him, his face all she could see, the emotions there on the surface. He convulsed and collapsed against her neck. Mallory wrapped herself around him and rolled to her side, still intimately joined with him, until his breathing steadied.

When he slipped from her at last, she protested, but he pulled her even closer, kissing whatever exposed skin he could reach.

So the first time hadn't been a fluke, a once-in-a-lifetime event. If her instincts could be trusted, it was a beginning like no other.

"I think," said a muffled voice into the pillow next to her ear, "I died and went to heaven. Are you an angel?"

"Well, I'm no virgin."

"That's a relief." His eyes crinkled and she marveled again at the honesty in their green depths. He stroked her hip with one hand, as though absorbing the feel of her skin through his fingertips. "You're amazing."

She smiled, a little wryly. "I bet you say that to all the girls the morning after."

"No." He touched her chin. "Normally I don't stay."

Their gazes met and held, breaking only when he leaned in the last couple of inches and kissed her.

"What's going on between us, Duncan?" she asked softly, when she could speak past the lump in her throat.

"I'm not sure." He paused. "All I know is, I started out working a job, and now I'm sharing a house and—at the moment—a bed with a beautiful woman who makes me crazy just looking at her. My brain doesn't have room for more than those facts just now."

Okay. No direct answer. She didn't want to ask why it left her feeling empty and unsatisfied. She had no right to feel that way. She watched him throw the duvet back and pull on his jeans again. Moments later the coffee grinder buzzed into action downstairs. She didn't have any answers herself. All she had was this lovely expansive feeling in her chest, the kind of feeling she got when she heard a beautiful piece of music or saw the light pierce the surf at a certain moment when the sun went down. A feeling of perfect happiness, one that came dangerously close to—

To what?

Just how happy did a woman have to be before she admitted that she'd just endangered all her dreams and hopes by doing something as crazy as falling in love?

13

DUNCAN HAD LIVED on the California coast for years, but he still couldn't get used to the thoughtless power of the breakers. Some guys, he knew, looked at them and saw a good day to surf. He looked at them and saw rocks pounded to particles and entire cliffs reduced to jagged geologic leftovers. The beach that formed Mallory's side boundary was wide and flat. Driftwood lay scattered on the sand like abandoned Tinkertoys, and ribbons of kelp lay drying in the sun as the tide went out.

For some reason, taking her hand as they walked slowly along the hard-packed, damp sand seemed even more intimate than the pleasure they had shared an hour ago. Strangely, he didn't mind. Her fingers clasped his hesitantly at first, then with confidence.

"Are you sure you should be doing this?" She lifted her face to the sun as the steady offshore breeze swept her hair back. "Shouldn't we be figuring out a way to shut down Blake Purdue and his operation?"

"We?" He paused. His instincts were at war with his inclinations again. One side cautioned him against telling her everything. He was ninety-nine percent convinced that she had no connection to Blake Purdue, either personal or professional.

But the last one percent niggled at him. She knew at least two of the couriers personally. She'd dated Purdue, regardless of her assurances that there was nothing going on.

But how could a woman who made love with such honest passion be anything but an ally? Could he really put the specter of Amy out of his mind, and once this case was over, maybe build something between them that could promise a future?

After last night, a future without Mallory in it seemed just as clean and windswept as this beach, but littered with things that were dead. If he didn't take this second chance when fate had been generous enough to give it to him, he ran the real risk of never coming alive again.

He swallowed, and made up his mind. "Maybe you can help me out here," he said. "How much do you know about computer manufacturing?"

If she had a problem with talking about work on a romantic beach, she didn't show it. In fact, he got the distinct impression she'd enjoy pitting her brain against any problem he could throw at her.

"I was on the software side, but I've been in lots of facilities. Ocean Tech, for example. They're not one of your victims, are they?"

"Not that I know of."

"So tell me, who's your client?"

"Your friend Barbara Mashita, at—"

"SiliconNext." He watched her process the information, and frown.

"When we ran into Purdue and Danny Barda at the

casino, I don't think it was an accident," he went on. "They had a meet set up. It was the only reason I could see to disappear the moment you and Carly were both on the dance floor. Not the actions of a guy looking to get lucky later on."

She gave him a disgusted look. "Not likely. Does that mean Danny is bringing him parts as well as Hope?"

"Yes. I've seen him." He hesitated a moment, watching her expression. In for a penny, in for a pound. He may as well give her the whole picture. "And my buddy Geoff tells me there have been some whispers about backroom gambling at the Lucky Miner. If you have a high-value commodity like those memory modules, you could exchange them for a lot of chips."

"I hate this. Hate it," Mallory whispered. "When he worked for me, Danny had a gambling problem. We had counseling as part of the benefits package, so I encouraged him to go through the program. Looks like he didn't." She sighed. "What can I do to help?"

"Whoa, slow down. You've already done your bit. I've been building up evidence and photographs, but they're not enough. Next step is to lean on one of the couriers on the way in. Get him to talk."

She stopped walking. "What does that mean? Rough him up? Aren't there laws against that?"

He grinned. "What's he going to do, call the cops?"

She dug her toes into the sand and stopped him. "You're not really going to hurt anybody, are you?

Danny, for instance? The guy is half your size, not to mention my friend."

"Of course not. I just have to present a more urgent threat than the one Purdue probably uses on him. Maybe I can use his friendship with you as leverage."

She gave him a long, level glance. "Does your mind work this way naturally, or did it take long years of training?"

He tried to find a grin, but it wouldn't come. "Both. I've been trained by the best." Denver. Amy. The years when he'd learned that the darkest view usually held the truth. The brilliance of the morning dimmed.

"I don't know if I like the sound of that. What happened?"

What if it were true what the shrinks said—that talking about something set you free from it?

"What is it, Duncan? Can you tell me?"

Could he? Would she understand how the memories popped up unbidden in his dreams, staining the way he saw people and relationships the way fingerprint ink stained clothing? The thought of revealing his humiliation stung. She'd never look at him in the same way again. The respect would fade from her gaze and he didn't think he could stand that.

"I'd rather not spoil the morning talking about it."

She hadn't moved. "You used to be a cop, didn't you? Before you became a P.I."

The sun glinted off the wet sand and a flock of sandpipers scattered as he moved toward them. "Are you sure you want to know about this?"

"I'm not going to pry, but I am ready to listen—and this beach is deserted."

He wanted to tell her, wanted to get it all out in the open. And if she got that look and suddenly remembered an appointment she had to go to, well, he'd just have to live with it. He'd lived with it before.

"Okay." They had at least half a mile of beach. His sad story wouldn't take that long. "You're right. Six years ago I was working narcotics for the Denver P.D. A coke case. We'd gotten far enough up the chain to know that a lawyer's office was actually a front for a ring of importers."

"Lots of high-profile people?" she asked.

"Yeah. Huge potential for scandal. At the time I happened to be involved with one of the lawyers. Amy Friedman. We'd been dating for a long time, long before I knew any of her associates were importing coke. I thought I knew her. Turns out I didn't."

"But how would she know anything about one of your cases?"

"Stupidity. I left something on my laptop and she found it."

"And she took it to these guys you were after?"

"Bingo. When you're in love, you trust the person. You don't expect them to go hunting around in your files for information they can use."

"What happened?" she asked so softly he could hardly hear her over the sound of crashing waves.

He shrugged. "What you'd expect. The whole operation crashed and burned."

"And then?"

His tone turned bitter. "And then my lieutenant asked for my shield. My partner's, too. Geoff knew about Amy and me and didn't report the possible conflict of interest, so I took him down with me. There wasn't much point in hanging around Denver after that. I headed west and kept going until that stopped me." He jerked his head toward the waves. "Otherwise I'd be in Siberia right now."

"I think you've been in Siberia for years. Honestly, Duncan, how were you to know?"

"Any cop with average intelligence would have broken off the relationship when he discovered her firm was involved."

"Is that a good reason to break up?"

"My lieutenant thought so."

"But if you love someone, you trust them, not suspect them. You expect them to be on your side. I would have done the same."

There was nothing quite as comforting as having someone you respect and maybe have feelings for tell you they would have done the same. It didn't take the sting out of the memory. But maybe he could work his way through the residual humiliation. Given a hundred years or so.

"So now you know the rest of the story," he said. "Time to turn around before we run out of beach."

"It turned out for the best," she said thoughtfully.

"I'm glad you think so."

His tone didn't seem to faze her. "You came out here and became a P.I. And then you walked into my yard and told everyone you were a contractor, you big liar." She kissed him. "Now you're stuck with it."

Hot damn. It felt good when she relaxed against his chest, her face in the crook of his neck. "I knew you'd get back to that," he murmured into her hair. "Do you ever not think about that house?"

"Sometimes. Like when you make love to me."

A devilish gleam lit her eyes and an answering grin started at the corners of his mouth. She looked around, wide-eyed with innocence.

"A morning off. And a deserted beach. Not a soul around. You could take my mind off it right now." One hand slid suggestively into the back pocket of his jeans.

It didn't take long to convince him.

HAPPINESS WAS so damn illogical.

Duncan counted lumber and shook his head. His case was still unsolved. It was lucky for Barbara he charged by the hour, not per diem. There was this porch, which had to be rebuilt by hand. And last but definitely not least, he'd seriously compromised his personal code of conduct and he didn't even care.

There were all kinds of reasons to be edgy and ready to bolt, and yet happiness permeated every cell in his body. The sun lay on his shoulders like an approving hand, and the jasmine rioting around the lower lattices of this tumbledown porch filled the air with the smell of summer. He had a feeling that from here on out, the scents of jasmine and coconut were going to bring Mallory vividly to mind.

He began to cut the new planks, welcoming the resistance of the dry fir and the bite of the saw. By midmorning he'd replaced the bad ones in the front, and had worked his way around to where piles of weeds told him Mallory had been gardening. Something cracked under his foot, and he shifted his weight just in time to stop his boot from going through the deck as the wood splintered under it. Thank God it had been him and not Mallory.

He bent and peered down into the hole. It looked as if the support beams for this section had rotted. A glance up at the corner of the house told him why. Water had probably been leaking out of the rusted downspouts for twenty years.

He lifted his head as he heard her call the cat from the back door. "Hey, Mallory. Come on over here." She rounded the corner and he held up a hand. "Slowly."

"Did you find some more rotten ones?" Her gaze dropped to the hole at his feet. "Oh. Guess so."

"I've got enough lumber for the floorboards, but it might take some real engineering underneath. I think you've got water damage."

"How do you know all this stuff?" she asked. "Does it come with the P.I. license?"

He circled around and joined her at the railing. His skin, his bones, ached to touch her, a silent imperative that prompted him to pull her against him and breathe deeply, his face close to her hair. "I had to work my way through college," he said. "You pick up a lot on construction sites."

"Looks like it's time for me to get some bids from a real contractor. No matter how multitalented you are, you can't do this by yourself."

"You like my talents."

Her smile turned impish, and her eyes took on a wicked glint. "Some women think those leather tool belts are a real turn-on."

"What do you think?"

"I like your undercover work." She kissed him, then danced away. "So you'd better get back to it, hadn't you?" She laughed as she went back into the house, and the corners of his lips twitched.

He'd better get down there and survey the damage so she had something to tell the guys when she called them for a bid.

A door about four feet high set into the lattice work on the side of the house swung outward reluctantly. The sun came through in a diamond pattern, hot flakes of light crossed by stripes of darkness. It was like trying to see by the flash of a strobe. The smell of dry dirt and old cardboard and rotting wood made him sneeze. Dead leaves that had blown under here during who knows how many winters crackled under his feet. The light glinted off broken glass near a pile of dusty Mason jars.

Great. Before the contractors got here he'd better muck out the place.

To his right, just inside the door, was a small suitcase. It was black, with a pull handle and wheels, and would probably fit neatly under an airplane seat. There wasn't a fleck of dust on it.

What was Mallory storing under here? It didn't seem right. Nothing else had been touched in thirty years, so surely she wouldn't put a single suitcase down here. She had three guest rooms to put stuff in. But she'd been working here yesterday. While he'd been occupied elsewhere, she could have shoved it in here and gone on with her weeding. But why do that?

Anomalies were his business. And the alarm bells going off in his head were never wrong.

He pulled his pocketknife out of his jeans and flipped open the can opener attachment. He inserted it in the zipper tab and carefully ran the zipper around its track. He didn't know whose fingerprints might be on the metal, but he was going to make sure they weren't his. He opened the lid and moved to one side, kneeling in the dry dirt and leaves, so the sun would strike the contents.

A long breath left his lungs.

Neatly packaged in protective pink electrostatic bags were at least a million dollars worth of memory modules.

14

DUNCAN TOOK THE STAIRS two at a time and Mallory crammed herself against the railing to give him room. "What's the hurry?"

He didn't even slow down. "Need the camera." He came out of the bedroom with it slung around his neck, screwing a smaller, more normal-looking lens on the front. A flash attachment poked out of his shirt pocket.

"What for?"

He gave her a brief glance, empty of teasing humor or desire or even simple friendship. It was the glance of a P.I. preoccupied with business. "To take pictures of those joists. So your contractors know what they're bidding on. I'll run to the mall after and get the film developed."

"But—"

Contractors didn't look at pictures. They came to the house and crawled around underneath it, muttering about freeze blocks and centers and code.

She began to get up. "Duncan, they won't—" Something tugged at her T-shirt and jerked her back down.

"Oh, no." When she'd squeezed to the side, she'd applied herself to the wet varnish on the spindles. "Damn, damn, damn!" She peeled her shirt away from the sticky stuff, leaving behind a nice swath of cotton lint that would have to dry and be sanded off. Again.

Calm down. It could be fixed. She had bigger things to worry about than gluing herself to the rail—her house could collapse on those rotted joists at practically any moment. He wasn't mad at her. Men got terse when they were concerned about something. And maybe he didn't know all there was to know about renovations. If he thought he was helping her by taking pictures, more power to him.

In the bedroom, she struggled out of the stained T-shirt and managed not to stick her hair to it as she pulled it over her head. The truth was, she was being selfish where Duncan was concerned. Desire and more lovemaking than she'd had in half a year had clouded her brain, obscuring the fact that the poor man was working himself to death for her.

She reached into a drawer and pulled out another top. Sure, he was being nice about it and pretending that working on her porch was some kind of cover, but she knew the facts.

Fact one: she was falling in love with him.

Fact two: she was getting too dependent on all the things he was doing for her.

Fact three: if she were ever going to be a whole person, to be more *her*, as he'd said, she wasn't going to do it by using the man, by letting him help her, by enjoying his company so much she forgot about developing the potential within herself.

In short, if she was going to realize the goals she'd

been so fierce about even a week ago, of becoming an independent person, able to stand on her own two feet and create a home for herself, she was going to have to help him get this investigation moving again. Once it was solved, they would see if what they had was real or just the result of two people living too close and playing one too many parts.

It hadn't felt as if anyone was playing a part last night, though.

She pushed that thought away and bent to replace the lid on the can of varnish. She carried the brushes downstairs, got them started in thinner and washed her hands.

He'd probably have a fit if she stuck her nose into one of his investigations. But he'd told her all about it. He had to have confidence in her. And sitting around watching people come and go wasn't getting him anywhere.

It would be perfectly normal for her to drop in on Blake. Even after the tension between them at the casino, he'd been as cordial as ever when she'd dropped him off. He'd even invited her in for a drink. He should be home from work by now. She'd pop over there, and maybe, if she got lucky, she'd see something that Duncan could work with to get things moving again.

She waited until she saw Duncan get in his car and leave for the mall. He'd be gone for a bit, so she had lots of time.

It seemed to take forever for Blake to answer his

door. When he did, he looked out cautiously and blinked when he saw her.

"Hi." She gave him her best smile, and he blinked again. His hand dropped away from the doorknob, and the door swung wider. She began to feel a little more hopeful, until she saw that his eyes were locked on her chest.

Oops. Maybe the orange tank top wasn't the best choice for an undercover job. Well, a woman worked with whatever weapons she had at hand. "Isn't it beautiful out?"

He nodded, looking a little dazed, and she stepped past him into the foyer.

"I was hoping you could help me."

His house was a lot smaller than hers, built sometime between the world wars. From where she stood, she could see all of the living room and into the kitchen at the back. To the right was a bedroom with the shades drawn and sheets tangled up on the bed. It was your typical bachelor place—or at least, what one was supposed to look like. Jon's immaculate condo didn't count. An average, normal guy lived here, going about his business of receiving stolen goods.

"Help you?" Blake echoed from behind her. "Looks as though you have plenty of help at your place already. You should have told me you were involved with someone, Mallory."

She thought fast. "I was afraid of losing your friendship." Private investigators probably had to make up their stories on the fly like this all the time.

"That would never happen. You know you can count on me."

He looked as though he was about to take her hand and squeeze it. "I know. It makes me feel safe, knowing that, Blake." She wandered back toward the kitchen, but if she'd hoped to see parts laid out on the table ready for shipment, she was disappointed. A half-eaten tuna sandwich sat on a plate next to a glass of beer. "Oh, dear, I've interrupted your supper. I'm sorry."

"It's okay. So what's he like, this guy?"

He's exciting, he's smart, and when he makes love to me, I lose my mind. This was one of those situations where the truth was far more socially unacceptable than a fib. She was beginning to understand the way Duncan thought. "He's nice, and he doesn't mind hard work."

Oops. Wrong thing to say. Blake bristled like Kiko did when she was offended. "I don't mind it, either. As I've proved already."

"I know, and I'm grateful. It's just that a woman in my situation..." Wary of gold diggers. Alone. Sexually starved. You know.

"You have to be careful, I know. Do you two go out much? Or is he a homebody like you?"

Aha. He was digging. Trying to see when he'd be rid of them, so he could invite some "friends" over? She'd fix that.

"He's a homebody. So refreshing in a man."

"But you ran into him at the casino," Blake objected. "Was he partying without you, or what?"

What was this, the third degree? She couldn't imagine what he was getting at. She needed to do what she came to do, and get out of here.

"Oh, no. We weren't as involved then as we are now." She clasped her hands in front of her, which had the effect of deepening her cleavage. Blake's eyes lost focus. "But I'm here for a reason. I hope you can help me. Kiko—my cat—she's gone. I'm just at my wit's end and don't know what to do. I know she comes over here all the time, so I was hoping you might have seen her. Otherwise, well, I don't want to think the worst, but..."

"When was the last time you saw her?" he said.

"Yesterday. She was sneaking across the road and I just know you put treats out for her. Don't you?"

"Treats?"

Mallory hadn't realized before the power a tank top could wield over a man. She was going to have to see if it worked on Duncan, too.

"Please, Blake. She has to be around here somewhere." There was no sign of stolen parts in any of the rooms she'd seen. "Maybe she got trapped in your garage when you came home?"

She reached back and turned the door handle that led to the garage. It opened under her hand. She stumbled, tripped over a chenille rug lying on the concrete in front of the door, and sprawled backward, her head winding up practically under the front bumper of his car.

"Jeez, Mallory, are you all right? Here, let me help you." He grasped both her hands and hauled her to her feet with such energy that she rocked forward and landed against his chest. His arms started to go around her when she caught her breath and wriggled out of his grasp.

"Wow, what a klutz I am," she said, breathless. He'd enjoyed that way too much. Time to go before he started getting ideas. She walked around the car and peeked under it. "Nope, she's not here."

Neither was anything resembling stolen parts, if you left out the taped boxes stacked up next to the car. However, they were neatly labeled with things like Football Stuff and Spark Plugs. Short of ripping one open, she'd have to believe it.

"I guess I'm just going to have to do a house-to-house canvass of the neighborhood," she said, practically skipping to the kitchen door and out to the front. "Thanks for your time, Blake."

"Hey, Mallory, wait a minute. If I see her, I'll bring her over, okay? And maybe I could bring some drinks or something at the same time."

"How nice of you." She made it to the front door and out onto the lawn. The soft summer air smelled so good she took a deep breath. "Bye!"

He probably thought she had a spring in her step. But it wasn't that at all. She was trying her best not to sprint flat out to the safety of her own yard.

"Men." Kiko was sunning herself on the back railing. Mallory scooped her up. "He couldn't care less if he'd shut you in his garage, could he, baby?" The cat wiggled out of her hands and jumped to the floor, shaking herself as if to rid her fur of any human touch.

"All he wanted was to cop a feel and ask me out again. But at least now we know more than we did before."

The next step was to see if Duncan was back and tell him what she had learned. It wasn't much, but sometimes an eliminated option was just as helpful as concrete evidence.

"Duncan?" She jogged around the side of the house. It was deserted, the only sounds the sigh of the breeze through the oaks and a pair of blue jays arguing somewhere above. A quick check of the deck told her he wasn't there, either, although the tools he'd been using were gone. Maybe he was in the garage. She swung the door open and the cool dark greeted her. Nothing here but her car. He must be in the house.

But no. She stood in the doorway of her bathroom and saw all her things right where they should be. Her robe hung on its hook, the towels lay undisturbed on their rods. The counter was clean.

In her room, the bed was just as it had been, tangled with the sweet energy of their lovemaking that morning. Her pictures stood on the dresser, the braided rug in front of the bed.

The temperature in the room seemed to drop twenty degrees. The black duffel bag was gone.

Broken ice particles seemed to be whirling through her blood, slowing her down, dragging time to a crawl as she leaned out the window. Like an answer to an unasked question, the street below was empty—no silver sedan sat between the plumbago bushes.

He hadn't gone to the mall. He'd packed up and left.

SERGEANT DAN STERN of the high-tech crimes unit stepped into Barbara Mashita's office and extended a hand. "Ms. Mashita."

"Sergeant. Thanks for acting so quickly on this. Hi, Duncan."

Duncan closed the door behind him and gave her a reassuring smile. "Good news." He indicated Stern's briefcase with a jerk of his chin. "I think we've got Purdue."

Barbara's eyes widened. "Sit down, please. How?"

Duncan glanced at Stern, who nodded a little stiffly. Duncan hadn't met a cop yet who was comfortable working with a P.I., but at least this one was willing to tolerate his presence on the case. The sheer scope of the conspiracy he'd uncovered was enough to make the other man overlook small details such as turf wars.

They sat on a low couch against the wall, and Barbara poured ice water from a carafe on the table in front of it.

Duncan spoke first. "Okay, from the top. I've got a couple of rolls of film showing Purdue and his couriers, but only a few shots that show any material being exchanged. I found his stash, so I've got pictures of that."

"Where were they?"

"Under a neighbor's house." The words tasted as bitter as a lie on his tongue.

"Another accomplice?" Barbara asked. "How many people are in on this?"

"We don't know." Stern put his glass on the table. "There's nothing to prove the neighbor was involved.

He could have been hiding the stuff there without her knowledge.''

Could have been. But they didn't know. That was the hell of it. Considering the money involved here, he couldn't take the chance that his heart had been right after all and she knew nothing about the suitcase under her porch. He had to go with what his head told him, which was "I told you so."

He'd made a fast departure with no explanation to get all the players in place before Purdue moved the stuff. As a result of which Mallory would probably never speak to him again.

"Did you bring them with you?" Barbara asked anxiously. "I can sign them back into inventory and nobody needs to know they were gone."

Duncan exchanged a glance with Stern. "No. I had to leave them where I found them. First of all, they're evidence. And second, if I move them, it might spook Purdue and he knows somebody—either me or the home owner—is on to him. He stops all operations and skips town, and we'll never catch him."

"Oh." Barbara's shoulders drooped with disappointment.

"I'll need you to identify as many of his couriers as you can." Stern picked up the briefing.

Barbara sank onto the couch, and Duncan handed her a manila envelope full of photographs. "We're saving the best for last. Sergeant Stern had an officer do a traffic stop this afternoon on Danny Barda and he was carrying a couple of modules, packaged in those pink bags. We'll need you to identify those, too."

Barbara got up and retrieved a pad of sticky notes

and a pen from her desk. "Okay. So obviously you know this is Danny Barda." She stuck a note on one of the pictures and wrote his name on it. "This is Hope LaCrosse, that's Chaz Reilly, and this one's Tim Barney. He's at a company over in Fremont now, but he used to work for me. Those are the only ones I know." Her voice wavered, and she swallowed.

Stern snapped open his briefcase and handed her a module in its pink wrapping. "What can you tell me about this?"

She took it with the care of someone used to handling high-value components and walked around the desk to the phone. She punched in two digits.

"Simon, it's Barbara. I need you in my office right away." She paused. "And Simon? Run."

Stern waited a moment while she disconnected. "As well as the parts, we succeeded in getting some information from Barda. Were you aware he had a gambling problem?"

"Gambling?" Barbara sounded as if that were the last thing she'd been expecting. "Danny is so poor he's sharing a two-room apartment with three other people. How can he afford to gamble?"

"That's just it. He can't," Stern said. "So when Purdue approached him with his scheme, he didn't have much choice. It was a way to clear his debts, but it also drove him in deeper with Purdue."

"He told us Purdue exchanges the modules for chips at the Lucky Miner casino downtown," Duncan added. "There's some kind of backroom black market, and he's in it up to his neck."

"And he's coerced my employees."

"I'm sorry, Barbara." The despondent look on her face practically forced the words out of him. He was going to have to work on his sense of detachment.

"Yeah. I am, too. Gambling." She sighed. "What's next?"

"We need to surprise Purdue with his hands on that stash before he takes it to his buyer at the Lucky Miner, if he hasn't already."

Her office door opened and a tall, slender man with a mop of curly hair practically fell through it, his chest heaving. He looked like a dandelion gone to seed. "What's going on, boss?"

"Simon, I need you to run this through the tester." She handed him one of the parts.

"I'll need to go with you. Chain of evidence." Stern got up. "Remember me, Mr. Martin? Dan Stern."

Simon nodded. "Come with me." As the door closed behind them, Duncan looked at Barbara and raised an eyebrow.

"Sergeant Stern made a presentation to my staff on high-tech crime a few weeks ago," she explained. "If that part came out of one of our testers, the system will recognize it, and we'll know someone from here took it. I guess we already know who."

In ten minutes, Stern was back in the office. "It belongs to SiliconNext." He placed the part back in his briefcase and snapped it shut.

Barbara exchanged a long glance with Duncan. "I guess that ties it up, then," she said.

"Except for a statement from Mr. Martin and from you, Ms. Mashita," Stern said. "I can take those now, if you have a few minutes."

"I do. Just let me see Duncan out."

He managed to keep a few steps ahead of her, but she caught up to him on the stairs to the lobby. "What's the hurry, Duncan? You owe me a shot of good cheer after all this bad news."

He could feel the No Trespassing look wash over his face. His features stiffened and Barbara looked a little surprised. "I thought it was pretty good news. We've got your crooks. Look, Barbara, I've got a lot to do in the next couple of hours." He didn't mean to sound gruff, but dammit, he had a job to do.

"I know you do. I just wanted to know one thing."

"What's that?"

"What about this home owner?"

"What about her?"

"How does she fit in?"

He felt almost sick. "We can't be sure. All I know is, she's a known associate of Purdue's, and the stuff was under her house."

"She didn't have to know about it."

"I know. But it looks bad." Stern had lifted a couple of prints off the handle of the suitcase. Duncan could only hope Mallory's weren't among them.

She said nothing for a moment. "Be careful. I wouldn't want an innocent person to get hurt."

Duncan didn't, either, especially if he'd put her in danger with his discovery.

He just wished to hell he hadn't glanced in his rearview mirror when he'd left and seen Mallory marching over to Blake's house like a woman on a mission.

15

THIS WAS WHAT HAPPENED when you threw your goals
overboard for the sake of a man. She should have been
true to herself and not let his green eyes and that smile
get under her guard and penetrate right to her heart.
He'd said it himself—she was becoming more *her*—
but was that because of her own efforts or because
she'd somehow found completion when she was with
him?

Now there was a scary thought. Next thing you
knew, she'd put on a frilly white apron and start worrying about waxy yellow buildup on the floors. If she
had floors. Mallory gazed at the particleboard in the
kitchen and tried to remember which day the floor
guy was supposed to come. Somehow it didn't seem
as important as it had been two weeks ago.

Duncan's case, apparently, was solved. That was
just dandy. There was nothing to stop her calling the
floor guy and getting on with her life.

Inexplicably, her eyes welled with tears, and she sat
down at the breakfast bar, shoulders slumped. Duncan could have at least said goodbye when he'd left
yesterday.

Or told her what he was doing.

Is that what detectives did? Decide a case was

solved and disappear from in front of windows all over America?

But how could he have decided the case was closed between one moment and the next? He hadn't even been working on it. He'd been under the house, worrying about rotting joists, and the next thing she knew, he was gone.

A rational man would have just called Barbara, reported in, and then the two of them could have figured out where their lives were going from here.

Now she was being irrational. Either she was going to be an independent woman, or she was going to pine after a man, forever feeling incomplete because he wasn't there. Which was it going to be?

Why did there have to be a choice? Couldn't a woman be herself and be with the man she loved, too? What was wrong with having it all?

The doorbell rang, and she banged her knee on the counter in her rush to answer it. Maybe it was Duncan. No, it couldn't be. He had no reason to ring doorbells anymore. Not after last night.

She swung open the door and Elaine breezed past her. "Hi, sweetie, how are you? I knew you'd be around. Where's the gorgeous Mr. Moore? I hope it's okay if the kids hang out in your trees."

In sheer self-defense, she filed her sister's questions like data cards and answered them in order. "I'm fine, he's not here, and of course it's okay."

"So where is he?" Elaine dumped her purse and a candy-pink plastic folder on the counter, then hitched herself onto the stool Mallory had just vacated.

Mallory glanced out the window to see Kevin and Holly attempting to scale a cedar, and got two bottles of strawberry lemonade out of the fridge. "Gone."

"When's he coming back? I want another look at that man. Anyone who can make Mother eat out of his hand is someone I want on my side."

"I don't know if he's coming back."

Something in her tone finally got through to Elaine. She stopped giving the new cabinets her critical eye and focused on Mallory. "Not coming back? Did you guys have a fight?"

She shook her head. "He was here this afternoon, working on the porch. I went to do an errand, and when I got back he was gone. He didn't even leave a note."

Elaine put her bottle down. "You don't want a note anyway. If they put it in writing, they really mean it. All this just happened today? Couldn't have. You look way too together."

"I don't feel very together. But give me some time and I will."

She expected a mom-type lecture of the I-told-you-so variety. But instead, Elaine leaned over and gave her a hug. Mallory relaxed on her sister's shoulder for a moment.

"You are together." Elaine's voice was firm, and Mallory sat up. "Mom told me herself that you've changed, and in a good way."

"Changed how?" If Mom said so, it must be true. Heaven knows her mother had been trying to change her for years, so she ought to know what it looked like when it happened.

"She says you've grown up. I'm not quite sure why she'd say that about a twenty-eight-year-old woman who's already made her millions, but who am I to quibble?"

"Anyone can make money if they have a product and someone to buy it. That doesn't make you an adult. Everyone at SpendSafe ran around in cutoffs and nose rings."

Elaine snorted. "Look at Jon. He turned thirty last year. He might think he's a vice president, but he's still twenty-one inside. Now, Duncan strikes me as a mature kind of man. He's got it together where it counts."

"Does he?"

Elaine shook her head. "If he doesn't, he gives an awfully good impression of it. From all the signs Tuesday night, I would have sworn he was crazy about you."

"So would I." She began to peel the label off the juice bottle.

"So what are you going to do about it?"

"I need to focus on my goals and remember why I got into this whole project. I'm tired of living in a construction zone. It's time to get serious about it and get it done."

Elaine eyed her. "That's commendable, but it's no answer. I think you deserve an explanation. Call him up. Ask him what the heck is going on."

Great. Easy for Elaine. She probably never had to

make such a call in her life. On the contrary; in college Elaine was always fending off calls from rejected lovers.

Mallory pushed the pieces of the label into a little pile and frowned. Why had she thought she'd known Duncan, had thought she'd seen some essential truth in him that had allowed her to trust him? All she knew was the story of his departure from Denver, and the fact that he hadn't talked to his mom in a couple of years. And all she had was his business card, sitting in a dish with a handful of screws and finishing nails.

"Mal? Yoo-hoo." Elaine waved a hand in front of her face. "Call him."

"I will. Today." Sure she would. "Hey, was there a reason you dropped over besides hoping the kids would get lost in the enchanted forest?"

"Yes, but I didn't want to be selfish if you wanted to talk."

"I'm done." That was the truth, in more ways than one. "What's up?" She lifted the juice and tried to swallow some of it.

"I finished that commercial script. I was wondering if you'd take a look at it."

So that was what was in the plastic folder. Mallory hoped she'd remember the kinds of let-'em-down-easy phrases she had memorized in the days when she was interviewing anxious software developers.

Elaine pulled out several sheets of paper and handed them to her. They were neatly formatted, exactly the way Richard liked them.

Mallory put her bottle down and scanned the brief

monologue once. Twice. Okay, so Elaine had forgotten to add the bank's boilerplate voice-over, and a couple of beats for the music. And it was probably five seconds longer than the twenty-five-second limit, but that was fixable. She read it aloud in her Bank Lady voice, and looked up.

Elaine's eyes were glowing in a way they hadn't since she'd seen her very first byline in the gardening section of the community rag, eight years ago.

"Wow. I read it out loud, but it didn't sound anything like that. It's really good, isn't it?"

The words had the Bank Lady's exasperated, comic tone down pat. All Mallory had to do was read.

"It really is. I'm going to fax it to Richard right now. Can you come up with more of these?"

"I wrote half a dozen, but this was the best one."

"Pick the top two, and I'll fax those over, as well. You may have noticed they've been playing the affair-in-the-teller-line one a lot lately. That's because they haven't been able to get a writer that makes him happy."

"That means a chance for me."

While Elaine waited anxiously behind her, Mallory wrote a note on a cover sheet and faxed the scripts to the number she knew by heart. One small step for Elaine could mean a giant leap for her sister's self-esteem, and Mallory was all for supporting that.

After Elaine had gone to locate the kids and load them in the van, practically hugging herself with anticipation, Mallory was alone again in the quiet of the house.

She gazed at the phone a moment, then picked up the receiver and dialed Duncan's number. She didn't even need the business card to remember it. *Don't make it sound as if it's important. This is just a business call.*

"Duncan, it's Mallory. Give me a call." She left her number and hung up.

The refrigerator hummed. A bird landed on the gutter above the kitchen window. Once, the solitude of the big, empty house had meant freedom and space. Lots of space, all her own, to recreate in her own image. She gazed at the moldings and freshly painted walls. There was independence and accomplishment in every brush stroke.

She needed to remember that. She had to stop looking for him in the spaces that had once been hers and that she now thought of as theirs.

There was irony for you. He'd moved in one room at a time, and now his smile and scent and energy had permeated them all. She was going to have to work to make the house her own again—if she even wanted to. What had started out as a crusade, full of passion and determination, had lost its savor somehow and become a huge mountain of jobs that would just have to be finished alone.

Maybe she'd been fooling herself all this time. Maybe independence without someone to share it with only meant loneliness.

Suddenly unable to sit still and listen to the fridge hum another second, Mallory walked out onto the deck. The hole in the planking gaped at her, and she hunkered down beside it.

How on earth had he decided he didn't need her or her window anymore? He'd been fretting about the joists. Over her shoulder, the sun moved another fraction in its journey toward the horizon, changing the slant of the beam falling into the hole. Something glittered in the dark.

She needed to do something with herself, even something as trivial as looking at what was under there. For all she knew, that glint could be water. Maybe there was a minor flood under her deck already.

She pulled the latticed door open and crawled in, expecting water up to her knees. As her eyes adjusted to the dark, she smelled nothing but dry dirt and old wood.

Broken glass. She thought back to the first night Duncan had arrived, when she'd been frightened by noises outside. He'd been unable to find the source of the sound of glass breaking. Maybe this was it. But how? Had an animal been trapped under here?

Her gaze swung from left to right, from light to dark. Not the sepia dark of forgotten storage, but the matte black of a modern suitcase. She had Coach leather luggage, bought in the days when stuff like that mattered. She'd never owned a black nylon carry-on.

Mallory sat back on her heels and replayed what must have happened. Duncan had been under here. He'd found the suitcase, opened it and seen what was inside. He hadn't been using his camera to shoot pictures of her joists. He'd been photographing whatever was inside that suitcase.

She crawled back outside and hunted around under the trees until she found a stick small enough to do the job. She'd watched enough episodes of *The X-Files* to know you weren't supposed to touch the evidence. She inserted the twig in the zipper tab and opened the lid just enough to see what was inside.

"Oh...my...God."

So much for trust and the fragile beginnings of love. She was looking at the end of whatever beginning she and Duncan had managed to create. One bad assumption was all it took to destroy it.

He thought she was in on some kind of conspiracy, hiding stuff for Blake Purdue. And she'd proved him right by running straight to his target, in a blaze-orange tank top that looked like a signal flag. He'd probably seen her waiting on his doorstep, just like one of his couriers.

It was a good bet the police were going to show up soon. How soon, she didn't know. Today? Tomorrow? The question was, what was she going to tell them when they did? She had nothing to do with Blake and his little army of thieves, but here was the suitcase, contradicting her.

What would happen if she moved it? Took it inside for safekeeping? No, bad plan. That would look even worse. A person might be able to claim ignorance of a suitcase under her porch, but it would look a little odd to claim she didn't know anything about the one sitting in her kitchen.

Mallory backed out of the dark recesses under the porch and emerged into the sunlight. She closed the lattice door and gazed at it. If Duncan could throw away something as special as what they'd shared over the past couple of days without even asking her for the truth or giving her the benefit of the doubt, who wanted him?

Not her.

Not very much, anyway. And she'd get over that.

Like maybe by the time Blake Purdue got out of prison.

16

DUNCAN SLIPPED through the darkness and paused behind a thicket of wild plums. In front of him, Mallory's untended lawn grew in hillocks and clusters of dandelions.

He had known he would be relegated to the edges of the action when the cops took over, but knowing something and liking it were two different things. Instinct told him that Purdue would move quickly. Danny Barda's limited knowledge about the operation had hinted that a big transaction was to happen soon at the casino. Barda had no idea when, but that suitcase had been full. It didn't take much to figure Purdue was probably ready.

Daniel Stern had hastily arranged a joint-forces effort with a detective named Will Keith from the Santa Rita P.D., but neither of them had arrived yet. As soon as Purdue picked up the goods, the plan was that the cops would tail him to the casino for the sale, where Stern's partner was stationed, warrant in hand. A good plan. Duncan shifted uneasily.

The only thing that could possibly go wrong was if Purdue showed and the cops didn't.

No. The only thing that could go wrong was if Purdue showed and the cops showed and Mallory walked out of the house, right into the middle of the stakeout.

Unease flickered in his gut. That was why he was really here, sitting in the bushes with bugs crawling down his neck. Normally, once he'd given a case to the city's finest, he'd dust off his hands and head back to his office to write up a final invoice. Not this time. This time, despite the cops' blunt instructions to stay out of the way, he was here...for Mallory.

A slice of moon dragged itself out of a bank of clouds and halfheartedly illuminated the leaves around him. The breeze off the ocean had died an hour ago, and now he could hear nocturnal creatures moving in the undergrowth.

Maybe it was Stern. He straightened slowly and scanned the untidy perimeter of the yard, but saw nothing. Probably a squirrel. With a sigh, he resumed his position.

In a perfect world, he'd have gone straight to her this afternoon and told her the bare outlines of the plan, then spirited her off to a bed-and-breakfast in Mendocino, whether she was still speaking to him or not. She could throw glassware at his head if she wanted, as long as it was far away from the action.

So far, Purdue had run a nice, quiet, nonviolent operation, accepting parts and raking in money without bothering a soul but Barbara and the other CEOs who had noticed problems. But the police couldn't take the chance that he wouldn't be willing to use force if he were threatened. Anyone would be capable of pulling a trigger if his multimillion-dollar operation fizzled because of an interfering neighbor.

So here Duncan was in the dark. He'd become good at waiting over the years. In this trade, patience was a prerequisite. But tonight the waiting was like insomnia without the comfort of a good mattress. His brain refused to shut off.

No matter how he tried not to think about it, the dark became a theater screen, bright with memory. Mallory on the beach, her forehead furrowed with concern and indignation on his behalf as he spilled the Denver story. Mallory silhouetted against the sun. Mallory in her mother's guest room, her head tipped back and her skin exposed to his hungry mouth.

His body tightened as if she were right there with him, a handbreadth away in the dark.

No. He'd think about strategy. He'd think about what would happen if and when Purdue came out of his house and crossed the street.

He'd think about what he'd do if the cops didn't show in time and he had to take care of this himself.

He wouldn't think about her laugh and her passion about this dumpy house and the way her unruly hair drove her nuts. He wouldn't remember how it felt under his hands, as soft and giving as she was. He wouldn't think about how he'd probably hurt her, or what would happen when this was over and he tried to explain. His body ached with the need to be close to her, not stuck out here in the dark with nothing to do but wait.

The fact was, he needed her, period.

And, true to form, he'd done his very best to chase her away.

Again the undergrowth moved. A branch thrashed, and with a sudden spurt of adrenaline, Duncan realized that what was approaching quietly across the grass was a lot bigger than a squirrel.

In the thin moonlight, he saw Purdue move cautiously across the open spaces, stepping from bush to bush on a diagonal from the road to the lattice door in the side of the house. He bent and pulled the door open, ducked inside and reappeared a second later pulling the suitcase.

Duncan wished he'd taken the time to invest in an infrared video recorder. All he had was a tape recorder in his pocket, and that wouldn't do him a damned bit of good. The cavalry, obviously, was not going to ride in on time to provide a corroborating witness.

And it was vital that the only other witness on hand stay inside, safely behind a locked door.

Please, Mallory. Tonight of all nights, don't come down to investigate.

Too late.

The back door opened and Mallory slipped out. She leaned over the rail and settled her forearms on it, as if she were doing nothing more than gossiping over the back fence.

"Hey, Blake. Out bird-watching again?"

Purdue jumped about six inches, and shot sideways like a crab before scrambling to his feet. "Mallory!" His voice cracked. "What are you doing here?"

Forget the cavalry. Duncan was on his own.

He pulled out the tape recorder, pressed the record button, and set it in the crook of a tree branch, fifteen feet from where Blake stood on the path.

Then he shifted his weight and crouched slightly, ready to spring.

"I live here, remember?" She indicated the suitcase with her chin. "Are you bringing me something, or taking it away?"

"What do you mean?" The handle of the suitcase ratcheted out of its housing with a sound like a shot. Duncan nearly leaped into the open. With an effort, he held himself back.

Blake stood the suitcase on its wheels and strolled slowly up the stairs toward her. Duncan's gut tightened with apprehension, and he cursed himself. He should have attacked. He should have ended it right here.

Stern, Keith—jump in any time.

The deck was wide enough for Mallory to skirt around Purdue, just out of arm's reach, and the latter had no choice but to turn and follow her back down to the lawn.

"You've been hiding your stuff under my porch since long before I moved in, right? I heard the noises, but never thought it might be you."

The bottom fell out of Duncan's stomach. *Don't confront him,* he prayed. *Don't push him.*

"I found them, you know." She pointed at the suitcase. "The memory modules. I'd be interested to know who you're selling them to."

"You would, would you?" Purdue said at last.

It didn't matter if his tape recorder wasn't the most expensive one on the market. Mallory's voice was clear enough to be heard across a courtroom. But why was she taking such a chance? Why was she telling him that she knew what he was up to? Did she have no idea how dangerous that was?

"Yes. I used to be in the industry, remember? I know them when I see them. What I want to know is, when do I get my cut?"

A wave of nausea rolled over him, and Duncan rocked back, flat on his heels.

This was why.

The only reason to spill everything he'd told her was because Purdue was no danger to her. Because there had been a tacit understanding between them all along.

Because his head had been right, and his heart wrong.

Again.

Purdue reached for the suitcase, as if to reassure himself it was still there, but his gaze never left Mallory. "Cut?"

She propped both hands on her hips. "Would you stop repeating everything I say? You've been using my house for a hideout for months, right? So I should be eligible for some kind of reimbursement. Rent, if you like."

Even at this distance, Duncan could hear the edge in her tone. It couldn't be fear. Not now. It must be anger. Annoyance at being left out of the deal.

Purdue eyed her. "I don't think paying rent to you counts as one of my expenses."

"I think it does. Come on, Blake. You could say we were partners, only I wasn't on board yet. But now I am. You've got a good thing going here. I could help."

"I don't need any help."

"I'd argue that one. You've got Danny Barda and Hope LaCrosse helping. Not to mention a bunch of other folks."

"How do you know?"

"I can't help it if people I know drop around to your house when I happen to be standing by the window. And I happen to see what they have in their pockets."

"You should mind your own business, Mallory."

"I'm hurt. Why don't you want to go in on this together? With everything I know, we could be a team."

Duncan glanced at the tape recorder, quietly doing its job. Her voice was as clear as one of her own radio performances. As if she—

He focused abruptly on the woman who was sabotaging his case.

Her voice.

Most people didn't speak that clearly in private conversations, never mind illicit conversations in the dark with criminals. Most people didn't know how to make their voices carry with no apparent effort. Actresses did, though. And so did radio talent.

A weight lifted off his heart, and he cursed himself for a fool.

It was a performance. The performance of a lifetime, and as far as she knew, there was absolutely no one around to hear it. Or to help. Mallory thought she was on her own, and she was doing everything she could to stall Purdue with his hands on the goods, just on the off chance someone would come in time.

Brave, crazy woman. The woman who challenged him at every turn. The woman he loved.

Loved, dammit! The last remnants of the doubt that had plagued him for the past couple of days, that had sickened him and kept him away from her every time he remembered that suitcase under her house, faded like fog under the warm glow of the sun.

The ghost of Amy laughed, deep in his memory, but it didn't have the same power over him it once had. The women were nothing alike. He could no longer sit meekly in the bushes when the woman he loved was in danger. He needed to prove to her somehow that his heart had been right.

Purdue's back was to the woods, and Mallory was facing him. Slowly, driven by the power of his sudden, irrefutable knowledge, Duncan moved into her line of sight.

Across the moonlit lawn, their gazes connected.

"There are people who would be very upset if they knew you'd been spying around," Blake said. "Does Moore know?"

She threw back her head and laughed, a sound of delight and relief that could be mistaken for derision if one didn't know better.

"Are you kidding? Of course not."

Duncan moved back out of sight, and Mallory's shoulders straightened with renewed confidence.

Purdue nodded. "Yeah, he's probably going blind from all the sex. He probably doesn't even know what these are." He gave her an angry look. "Now is a fine time to talk about partnerships. You should have gone out with me when you had the chance."

She shrugged. "I respect your mind. I think we'd make better business partners."

Now Duncan recognized the edge to her voice. It was anger. She was furious with Purdue for doing this to her. *Don't let it show, Mallory,* he thought. *Hang on. Just until he gives me a break.*

"I already have partners. I don't need you for that."

"Yeah? Who are they?" When he stayed silent, eyeing her, her body language became playful. The bimbo in over her head. "I already know everything. You may as well tell me. Does it have something to do with the casino? You know, where we met Danny that night?"

"Not much gets past you, does it? You need to stop asking questions."

"Oh, come on. I heard a rumor that you can trade hardware for chips there if you know the right people."

"I know that you're too nosy. Maybe if you don't keep quiet about this, bad things will happen."

"Blake." The look from under her lashes was reproachful. "How can you say that? I thought you liked me."

"Yeah, I like you. That's why I'm warning you. Too many people have too much invested in this for you to go shooting your mouth off. Clear?"

"What would you do to me?"

"Maybe there would be a fire. Too bad, after all your hard work. Maybe you wouldn't make it out. It's hard to say. In fact, maybe you should come with me and talk to them about it."

Before Duncan could move, Purdue had snaked out a hand and grasped her arm. With his other hand, he grabbed the handle of the suitcase and began to drag them both along the bumpy path.

At the moment her performance ended and real fear set in, Duncan leaped out of hiding.

"Let go of her, you bastard!"

Blake whirled around, his mouth open in surprise.

MALLORY DODGED SIDEWAYS as two dark, burly shapes darted out of the trees and jumped on Blake. But it was just like him to try to run and drag the suitcase at the same time, instead of cutting his losses and leaving the goods behind. When the thrashing bodies finally separated, a big African-American guy had Purdue in a death grip with his wrists pinned behind him, and the other, skinnier one had taken custody of the suitcase.

Duncan materialized out of the dark and wrapped an arm around Mallory, pulling her to safety near the kitchen steps.

The man with the suitcase looked at them as he followed Purdue and his captor toward the street. "I'll be back for statements once we finish up at the casino," he called. "Don't leave."

Duncan waved in acknowledgment and ushered Mallory up the steps and into the safety of the house.

"Are you all right?" His voice was rough with concern and the dregs of fear. To her, it sounded like music.

"Yes. He didn't hurt me. Were those the cops?"

"Finally. I swear I aged ten years in the last ten minutes." He released her and leaned heavily on the counter. "Please don't ever do that to me again. I had no way to get you out of the way if things got nasty when they took him down."

Cold reality rinsed away the hopeful illusions that had just begun to warm her heart. Duncan hadn't come back in the nick of time to say he was sorry, or to save her from Blake's nasty cronies. His duty had been to get her out of the line of fire, and he was annoyed with her for making it difficult.

He was putting on another face, and she'd fallen for it. Again.

"That was your part of the job?" she asked. "To get me out of the way?"

She had once thought disappointment was a mental thing. Now she knew differently. It settled in her bones, taking the starch out of her spine, making her arms and legs feel heavy.

"No," he said. "Once the cops get involved, I'm out of it. Case closed."

"Then what are you doing here?" Why wouldn't he go play with his cop friends, so she could crawl upstairs and cry for a month? "You left because you thought I was renting my porch to Blake Purdue. I practically risk life and virtue to go over there and look inside his house to see if he's got the parts there, and by the time I get back, you're gone. No 'I trust you, Mallory,' no 'Let's talk about this,' no nothing. Then I found the suitcase and I knew why." Her voice threatened to break and she stopped before she completely humiliated herself.

"I didn't want to think you were involved." He sat heavily on one of the counter stools.

"Gee, that makes such a difference."

"I couldn't take the risk. And—" he paused, took a breath, and went on "—and the scenario was so close to what had happened with Amy that it was too easy to make a mistake."

She waited.

"I mixed her up with you in my mind. That was wrong. You aren't the same. The situations are nothing alike. I should have realized that right away." There was sincerity in every husky word, every scratched vowel that told her his throat was constricted with emotion.

"When did you change your mind?" she asked finally, when the silence became too agonizing to stand.

"Sitting out there." He indicated the dark beyond the window. "When I realized what you were trying to do, you got me right in the heart."

"And what is your heart saying now?"

He slid off the stool. She tried not to lean against him, but it was hard when his arms were so tight around her. So warm. So safe.

"It's saying, 'Moore, you dummy, this woman is

one in a million. This is the real thing. Don't screw up.'"

"It has a way with words." She looked up. "The real thing, huh?"

"Yeah." His voice was soft, husky. As though he were about to kiss her. "I hope you feel the same way."

She was so mesmerized by his eyes and the shape of his mouth, just inches from her own, that she temporarily forgot how to form words. They were unnecessary, anyway. Her body was doing all the speaking.

He pulled her into his arms and kissed her, a deep, searching kiss that spoke volumes about the depth of his feelings and how close they could have come to losing each other. There was truth in that kiss. Truth and reality and stark, honest need.

An eternity later, during which her entire world tilted on its axis and then righted itself, he pulled away a fraction to look into her eyes.

"Tell me what made you go out there and confront him. I swear, when I saw you come out on that porch, I thought my heart would stop altogether."

"I was angry."

The expression in his eyes sent a sizzle down her spine. "Speaking strictly from my selfish point of view, that's not a very good reason to take on a criminal, at night, alone."

"I was really, really angry. I heard him out there and I wanted answers. So I set my answering machine to Audio Record and took it out on the deck. With any luck it taped our whole conversation. We can give it to the cops when they get back."

The laugh lines at the corners of his eyes deepened as he smiled. "Along with the one I have running in your crepe myrtle. Between the two of them we should have enough evidence to prosecute. I'd say you were more than a match for him." He sobered. "Let's get a few things straight. I don't want to be the guy out in the dark anymore. I want to wake up in the morning with you beside me. I want to share mornings. And noons. And nights." His voice got a little husky on the final word.

That was pretty straight, all right. No room for doubt there. Her heart swelled with joy. Not with illusions this time. The real thing.

Epilogue

CARLY LOUNGED on the newly painted deck rail, one bare leg swinging lazily, and sipped a glass of iced tea. Mallory eyed the rail, but the contractors had assured her it was better than new, now that the rotted timbers had been replaced.

"I heard your new ad on the way over," Carly said. "It sounded good. They finally found a writer?"

"You'll never guess. My sister." Mallory smiled.

Carly's leg stopped swinging. "Elaine wrote that? Since when did she get into radio?"

"Since about a month ago. Richard loved her spots and bought three of them. So he's happy, Elaine's happy, and the bank's happy, which makes me happy."

"That ain't all that's making you happy, *mija*. I've never seen you glow like this before. It can't be just hard work. It must be lots of great sex."

She laughed. "It must be. But don't tell my mom. She's still convinced Duncan is a gold digger, lying around the house eating chocolates and living off my money."

"She would think that if you married the president of a bank. But she'll get over it." Carly paused and reconsidered. "Maybe."

"She'd better. Guess what I got last night."

"What, besides thoroughly—"

Mallory flashed her left hand. Carly squealed in midsentence and grabbed her fingers, where a modest diamond twinkled and shone. "Oh, *mija*. Congratulations." She hopped down off the rail and enveloped Mallory in an exuberant hug. "I'm so happy for you."

."You're going to be my maid of honor, right?"

Carly pulled back in surprise. "Not Elaine? Shouldn't it be your sister?"

"She's changed, Carly. She doesn't have to be the center of the drama anymore. Maybe it's the radio exposure."

Carly squeezed her again. "I would be delighted and honored, *amiga*. Who's best man?"

"Another guess. How is it going with you two?"

Carly shrugged and her smile dimmed. "We have things to work out. Not that the sex isn't terrific, mind you," she added hastily. "But Geoff's a lot older than I am and my brothers have this thing about him being an ex-cop and...you know. When we stumble out of the bedroom we have to deal with real life. But I promise you, at your wedding everything will be perfect."

She snagged her handbag off the makeshift table the contractors were using for the table saw. "We need to get together and start making lists and things. But right now I've got to hustle. I've got a job interview and I can't go in shorts."

"You've got me down as a reference, right?"

"Never fear. Talk to you later...and congratulations again and again."

Carly drove off and Mallory collected the glasses and wandered inside. She heard Duncan's voice on the phone upstairs and, like a metal filing to a magnet, felt the pull beneath her ribs that drew her close to him. He smiled at her as she stood in the bedroom doorway, and held out one arm. She snuggled under it as though she'd come home. In a few moments she realized he was talking to Barbara Mashita.

"How soon will you have to testify at the trial?" Duncan asked. "Don't worry, it's pretty straight-forward. What did they wind up charging Purdue with? I know they offered him a deal if he'd give them his buyer at the casino. He rolled over like a puppy."

He paused to listen, then covered the receiver and whispered to Mallory, "Grand larceny and criminal possession of stolen property. We won't have Purdue as a neighbor for long."

He turned his attention back to Barbara. "What about Danny Barda and the other people? That, plus burglary, huh? So you went through with the charges, even though he and his sister had no choice? I know, Barb. You didn't have a choice, either. Maybe the judge will be lenient because it's his first offense, and it was clearly extortion. Well, I'm glad you told me. Take care of yourself." He laughed. "Right. I could do with a rest between your cases." Still smiling, he turned off the phone.

"Like for a honeymoon." He pulled Mallory closer and nuzzled her neck, but she wriggled away.

"I think you have one more call to make," she reminded him.

"Can't it wait?" Duncan reached for her again, but she snatched up the phone and handed it to him. He stared at it as though it would give him the right words.

"If not now, when? The night before we get married? I don't think so. Besides, I know you want to."

"Yeah, I do." He flashed her a smile that warmed her right down to her toes, and punched in the 303 area code.

The phone rang on the other end. "What if she's not— Oh, hello. Mom? No, I'm fine. How are the girls? That's great. Listen, Mom? I've got some news for you." Mallory had to smile as he made patting motions in the air with one hand. "Mom, no, it's okay. I'm not in the hospital. I'm not dead. Would you listen?" He rolled his eyes in mock despair.

Mallory laughed and wrapped both arms around his waist.

"I hope you guys are going to be around on the weekend. Kari and Jen, too? Great. We've got tickets booked to Denver Thursday. We'll be at your place around five o'clock." The phone squeaked a single syllable, and Duncan grinned. "Yes, you heard that right. *We.*"

Duncan looked deep into Mallory's eyes as he spoke, and she knew he'd found the words. They came straight from his heart.

"There's someone I want my whole family to meet."

Mallory wondered if it was possible for one person to hold this much happiness. Maybe not.

Maybe happiness, like making love, was meant to be shared between two.

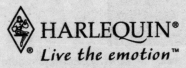

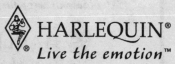

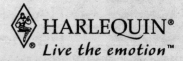

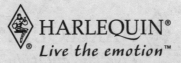

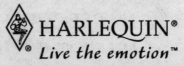